Unraveling Darkness

Dar
Bo
Mar

Copyright © 2017 Marissa Farrar
Warwick House Press
All rights reserved

Edited by Lori Whitwam
Cover art by Covers by Combs
ISBN-13: 978-1979957724
ISBN-10: 197995772X

For my Marley-love

Always missed

Chapter One

"Four, nine, two, zero, six, three, seven, one, eight, five."

I stood in the cabin, with the five men in front of me, and told them the code which would unlock the memory stick my father had died trying to protect. As I spoke, each of the digits appeared in front of me, flashing with the luminescence I always saw when one number was trying to speak louder to me than another. I hadn't yet told the guys about my spatial sequence synesthesia, but I figured there was still time.

It seemed like such a simple thing to be able to work out, ten random digits between zero and ten, but there was a one in one million chance of anyone guessing the number. One million different variations of ten digits between one and ten landing in a certain order. And if anyone tried to input that number incorrectly, the contents of the memory stick would be wiped.

I looked around at each of the five guys, trying to judge their reactions. My gaze went to Isaac first, the leader of the group and the one who made the decisions. Beside him stood Clay, his head tilted to one side as he regarded me, his jaw-length blond hair falling over his face. Lorcan sat in a chair, the pain caused from having been shot back at the house only serving to deepen his brooding attitude. He currently wasn't wearing his usual leather jacket, and the multiple tattoos running down his arms and up the side of his neck looked out of place without it. Kingsley, despite the huge muscles, was the thinker of the group and sat at the table with his fingers pressed to his full lips, his eyes, so dark brown they were almost black, fixed on my face. Lanky, blond Alex—the medical doctor—watched me with what appeared to be amusement.

None of them seemed angry with me for only now revealing I knew the code, though I'd lied by telling them I hadn't remembered yet. That had been the thing I had been most afraid of—that they'd reject me for having withheld the truth.

No one said a thing, and my nerves increased, fluttering up through my stomach to condense in my heart, making its beat trip. I willed someone to break the silence so I could face whatever I had coming.

I looked back to Isaac, knowing he'd be the one to lead the way.

Fine lines appeared between his brows, and he pressed his lips together. "You're sure?" he asked.

The white shirt that normally would have gone beneath a suit jacket, but which he'd obviously not bothered to grab when we'd been under attack at the house, was crumpled and blackened in places from the smoke. That morning's stubble roughed up his jaw. He was normally so clean cut, and I thought I kind of liked this more rough and ready version of Isaac.

My body still hummed from what he'd done to me, but strangely I didn't feel embarrassed or humiliated. Instead, a spark had been lit inside me, and I was filled with the sensation of being wanted, needed, of belonging to something bigger than myself.

I dipped my chin in a nod. "One hundred percent." My lips parted, words dancing on my tongue. Would now be the right time to tell them about my synesthesia? It would convince them of my ability to remember the code correctly. But I had more pressing matters at hand. The reason I hadn't revealed the code right away was because I'd worried about what would happen to me once I had. The only reason the guys had taken me in the first place and then kept me safe, was to get that code. Now they had what they wanted, and I was no use to them anymore.

I glanced across the room toward the others, checking if they were following Isaac's lead. Clay stood with one ankle hooked over the other, and his arms folded across his chest. He gave me a small smile that told me I'd done good, then threw me a wink that I doubted any of the others would have noticed. Lorcan remained in the chair. He'd put on his shirt after Alex had patched him up from the gunshot wound, but I knew the bandage was hidden beneath the material. Lorcan had never been the chilled, easy-going one, and now the physical pain he carried had hardened his features even further, but he dropped his chin in a nod of acknowledgement to me.

Kingsley was the one, other than Isaac, that I'd felt the worst about lying to. He'd worked with me to bring back my memories of the night my father had died, and I felt horrible that I'd lied to him, making him believe we hadn't achieved the one thing we'd set out to do.

"Why didn't you tell us before?" Alex's blond eyebrows pulled together, and his teeth captured his lower lip in concern.

"I was worried about what you all would do with me," I admitted.

He shook his head—a tiny movement that almost didn't happen. "Do with you? What did you think we'd do with you?"

I shrugged. I didn't know. In my darkest moments, I'd believed they might have had me killed, but it felt crazy to think that now, though at the time I'd had every reason to. These men had kidnapped me, and even if they'd done it for the right reasons, it wasn't as though they'd acted like knights in shining armor. No, they'd done what they'd had to. And I'd done what I believed *I'd* had to during that time, too.

But the question still remained. Now they had the code, what was going to happen to me?

Nerves fluttered inside my stomach, like moths batting mindlessly at an outside light in the dark. I didn't want to ask the question, but I had to know.

"What happens to me now?"

Isaac frowned, his head tilting to one side. "What do you mean?"

I dug my teeth into my lower lip, nipping at dry skin, before speaking. "You have what you wanted, so what are you going to do with me?"

His green eyes narrowed. "What do you *want* us to do with you?"

"I don't know." That was what I said out loud, but inside I was thinking I wanted him to repeat what he'd just done to me, with all the guys watching. I wanted him to make me feel that way again, and then I wanted Clay to take his turn, and then Alex, and Lorcan, and Kingsley. I wanted to belong to each of them, and I wanted the others there while it happened. It was crazy and hedonistic, but they'd made me feel a part of them, and I didn't want that to end.

"If you go home," Alex said, straightening, "you'll still be in danger."

I nodded. "I know, but Aunt Sarah might also be in danger."

"You're more important to us than your aunt." Kingsley folded his arms across his massive chest, and I flashed a smile across at him, thanking him silently for telling me I still mattered, even though they had what was in my head.

Isaac's features tightened. "We won't let anyone hurt you, Darcy, not Hollan, or anyone else, for that matter." His words sent a frisson of emotion I couldn't quite analyze through me.

"Thank you, but it's not that easy for me. My aunt took care of me after my father died. She's the only one who's ever been there for me, and she could have walked away so many times when I was a teenager, and I was the most horrible person in the world to her, but she didn't. She stuck by me, and I owe her." I took a breath then added, "Besides, she's the only family I have."

The men exchanged glances then Isaac's shoulders softened. "Getting to your aunt won't be easy," he said. "You understand that, don't you? Hollan is going to realize she's the first person you're going to reach out to if you can. He's going to have her surrounded by watchdogs, even if she doesn't know it."

I pressed my lips together and nodded. Of course, Isaac was right. They'd already warned me of this once before, and I hadn't listened. I'd gone ahead and done what I'd wanted, and Hollan had found the house and tried to kill everyone inside. It suddenly occurred to me that Hollan wouldn't have wanted me killed. No, what would have happened to me would have been much worse. He'd have taken me and tortured the code out of me. Would I last under torture? I'd like to think I'd have been strong and refused to give the number to him, no matter what he did to me, but truthfully, I couldn't say what I would do. It was easy to be brave and stand by your morals when you felt relatively safe; it was a whole other thing when your father's murderer was tearing off your fingernails with a pair of tweezers.

My thoughts must have caused the blood to drain from my face, as Isaac frowned then reached out and lightly touched my fingers with his. "Darcy, what's wrong?"

I shook my head. "Nothing. Just my overactive imagination."

The concern didn't leave his face. "As long as you're sure."

I nodded. "I'm sure."

"Okay, so say we manage to extract your aunt, we can find somewhere safe for both of you to go until all of this is done with."

Even though I'd only just been imagining how it would be if Hollan tortured me, I shook my head. "No, I want to see Hollan dead. He killed my father. I have the right to exact my revenge."

Alex stepped forward. "That's not a good idea, Darc. If anything goes wrong, Hollan will be able to get the code from you."

I gritted my teeth. "Nothing will go wrong."

He fixed me with his cool blue gaze. "You don't know that."

"I'll have the five of you with me. You'll make sure nothing goes wrong." Was I being selfish saying that? Was I putting them in a more vulnerable position by asking them to do this? Maybe it would be better if I hid away with Aunt Sarah and let them deal with things, but that wasn't the type of person I was. I needed control, and besides, my father had given *me* the code, not anyone else. It was me he'd entrusted with it, and I couldn't just hand everything over to someone else to see through.

I wanted Hollan dead, and I wanted to know what was on that memory stick. It had been important enough for my father to die for, and now we had all these men willing to sacrifice their lives to either protect what was on it or get access to that information.

"Before we can do anything else," Isaac said, "I need to make contact with base and let them know what happened and that we're still alive. News will have gotten back to them that the house has been razed to the ground, and they need to know we made it."

Who were they? The people Isaac and the others worked for?

Isaac continued. "If they think we're compromised, they might pull us off the job."

Alex looked at him with a frown. "Compromised?"

"Yes, because of Darcy calling her aunt. You know he's not going to be happy about it."

Clay shoved his hands into his pants pockets and joined in the conversation. "We can explain it was a mistake and she didn't understand what the repercussions might be."

Isaac shrugged to show it didn't matter what I'd understood. "Even so, if he thinks another team will do a better job, you know he can pull us off this one and put another team in place."

I looked between the guys. "No, they can't do that!"

Kingsley nodded. "I'm afraid they can."

I didn't want anyone else taking their places. What would happen to me then?

Lorcan spoke from the couch, his voice gruff from the pain he must still be in. "We could always lie. We don't tell the boss about how Hollan found the house. He's got no way of knowing. If Darcy hadn't admitted to the phone call herself, we'd never know now, we'd just be making guesses."

The men exchanged glances.

Alex shrugged. "Lorcan has a point."

Isaac's hand went to his mouth, and he rubbed his fingers across his lips as though wiping something away. It was the same finger that had been inside me, and with a thrill, I wondered if he could still smell me on his skin. "And if he finds out the truth?"

"He won't. None of us will tell him, and I'm sure Darcy won't."

I shook my head. "I won't say a word."

I wondered who this 'he' was they were all talking about. He was obviously their boss, but was he also the same person who'd taken them from their foster care homes when they'd been children? Did they resent this man for that, taking away their only chance at the possibility of finding a family to adopt them so they could go on to live normal lives, or were they thankful they'd escaped the system and gone on to live far more exciting lives than a regular adoption would have ever given them? Did they see this man as a boss, or did they see him as a father figure? I made a mental note to ask the guys how they felt about their upbringing when I managed to get each of them alone.

"Even if we keep our mouths shut," Kingsley said, "he might still find out. If we take Hollan into custody, Hollan himself might tell him."

"I don't want Hollan to live long enough to say anything to anyone," I bit out, sudden anger flaming hot inside me.

Kingsley shook his head, and I saw pity in his deep brown eyes. I'd found all the men intimidating when we'd first been acquainted—of course, I had, I'd been kidnapped by them. Kingsley had been so big and determined, forceful even, but he'd surprised me with his tenderness.

"That might not be your choice," he said. "We think Hollan is at the top of the food chain when it comes to the memory stick, but there may be others. We don't want to chop the head off this one, only to find another grows back in its place. Just getting the memory stick and killing Hollan might not be the end of it. Others could still come after us, determined to get the drive back."

Isaac raised a hand to bring him to a halt. "Speculation isn't going to get us anywhere. But I agree that we don't admit we know how Hollan found us in order to protect Darcy and this mission. Do we all concur?" He looked around the group. One by one, they each put up a hand.

"Agreed." Alex raised his hand into the air.

Kingsley copied his motion. "Agreed."

"Agreed," Lorcan said, "but I'll keep my hand down if that's okay."

Isaac nodded. "Of course." He looked at Clay.

Clay lifted his hand. "Sure, man. Agreed. Anything for Darcy."

I gave him a grateful smile. I could hardly believe they were all doing this for me. The last thing I wanted was for any of them to get into trouble, but they must have seen something in me as well, or surely they'd just tell their boss the truth and have me shipped off to wherever they needed people to go to keep them safe.

"Thanks, guys." Heat crept up my throat. Crazy how having them all watch me orgasm didn't make me feel anywhere near as self-conscious as having them being nice to me.

How many kinds of fucked up was I?

Chapter Two

"I need to get to the satellite phone," Isaac said, "and call this in. Leaving out the part about Darcy phoning home, of course."

He shot me a frown, showing his displeasure at having to lie. I didn't blame him. I wouldn't want to lie either, especially not for me. But he was doing it, even though I knew he didn't want to, and somehow that meant even more.

I thought of something. "Why do you need a satellite phone? What happened to your cell phones?"

"We had to destroy them. Once our location had been compromised, we needed to get rid of anything that might be linked to the house. There will be more here, but until we can be sure we're safe, I'll stick to the satellite phone. Besides, in case you hadn't noticed, this place is in the middle of nowhere. We don't exactly get great cell coverage."

My mind went to other ways we might be traced. "What about the vehicles outside?"

His gaze flicked toward the small window of the cabin. "Yeah, that's always a risk, but the other two cars parked outside of the house were acting as decoys, so if trackers were put on anything, it would have been those, not the vehicles we'd hidden between the trees."

My teeth grated on my lower lip. "Hollan and his men know which vehicles we've got now though, don't they? They chased us while we were in them."

Isaac aligned himself in front of me and put his hands on my shoulders. "They're not going to find us here, Darcy," he said, obviously picking up on the reasons for my anxiety. "This place is in the middle of nowhere. Unless you know exactly where it is, you're not going to find it."

I remembered how, on the way here, I hadn't seen any signs for towns or anything else, for that matter. I hoped he was right. The thought of Hollan and his men descending upon this little place filled me with fear. It was one thing being in the big house with its hidden escape routes and weapons, but the cabin was only a matter of one floor and a handful of rooms. I struggled to imagine how safe we'd be here if someone decided to attack.

I guessed I didn't have much choice but to trust him.

Isaac stepped away from me and moved to the front of one of the couches, where there was a woven rug on the floor and a pine coffee table on top of it. He lifted the coffee table with ease and placed it to one side, off the rug. Kingsley stepped in to help him, and the two of them crouched at one end of the rug and started to roll. I watched, confused at what was going on. They rolled the rug to the end, revealing a square cut into the middle of the wooden flooring. I understood what I was seeing—a cellar trap door that had been hidden from immediate view. Both Isaac and Kingsley got their fingers under the edges and pulled up. That portion of the floor lifted, revealing a hole underneath, and I could just see a kind of combination of steps and a ladder underneath, leading down to a space hidden beneath the cabin.

Without another word, Isaac stepped down into the hole, disappearing gradually as he took each step downward. When he was down, Kingsley lowered the hatch, but the rug and coffee table remained where they were.

I stared at the spot Isaac had just vanished into. "What's he doing down there?"

"Making contact with the mother ship," called Clay. He bounded to his feet and headed into the kitchen. "Now, let's see what supplies this place has. I could eat a scabby horse."

I wrinkled my nose at his description. "Hey, can you point me in the direction of the bathroom?"

"Sure, it's that door over there." He pointed to one at the back of the cabin. "We don't have to worry about you trying to escape through the window or anything, do we?"

"I think my escaping days are over."

He grinned. "Glad to hear it."

I headed to the bathroom. It was a good size and clean, and there was a window, but I had no desire to attempt to climb out of it. There was also a deep tub, and I looked at it longingly. What I'd give to lounge in hot water full of bubbles for an hour or longer. My body still ached from everything I'd been through. But I didn't want to look or act like a princess—no matter what Lorcan's pet name for me might be. I wanted to stand beside the guys as their equal, and they'd never see me that way if I lazed around when there was important work to do.

Between my thighs still felt slick from Isaac's fingers. I wanted to clean myself up and go back out there feeling stronger. I used the toilet and wiped myself clean, then went to the sink to wash my hands and face. I looked up into the mirror to see a wild-eyed woman looking back. My blonde hair was in tangles around my face, and smudged shadows hollowed beneath my blue eyes. Did I look older than I had a few days ago? Harder? Maybe I'd lost a couple of pounds, and it showed on my face, or maybe it was getting shot at and having to run for my life that had caused the change.

I exhaled a shaky breath and clutched the edges of the sink. My experiences over the last few days flooded over me, hitting me like a sudden wave that took my feet out from under me and sent me spinning. The world suddenly seemed further away, as though I wasn't quite connected to anything, and the feeling unnerved me. My heart pattered, and my mouth ran dry, and I squeezed my eyes shut, trying to hide from everything. Was this how it felt to have a panic attack? I wanted the guys to see me as strong, not weak, and I fought against my body's reaction.

Kingsley's deep, melodic voice sounded in my head. *Control your breathing. Breathe in slowly through your nose and out through your mouth. Feel yourself start to relax...*

I did as the imaginary Kingsley told me, and the world around me started to right itself again. The feeling of the world spinning began to slow until eventually the floor solidified beneath me.

When I felt strong enough, I opened my eyes, though I continued with my breathing. I was tough enough to handle this, I told myself. Plus, I had five men out there who were willing to help me.

It occurred to me that killing Hollan and retrieving the memory stick might only be the start. Finding out what was on there—information important enough for my father to risk everything to protect—might send my world spiraling in a whole new direction.

Not wanting to think about that too much, I ran the faucet, filling the sink up with hot water and soap, then set about cleaning myself up. I washed my face and my body as best I could with the water and a small hand towel. When I was done, I tucked Alex's shirt into the waistband of my jeans, so it didn't look quite as billowy on me. I wished I had my own clothes, but under the circumstances, I didn't think I could complain that I wasn't overly keen on my outfit.

I left the bathroom and went out into the main living area of the cabin. It was strange to think of Isaac doing something beneath our feet. I looked around to the others. Lorcan was still in the same position on the couch. I wondered if Alex had given him any more painkillers yet, though Alex was nowhere to be seen, so perhaps that was what he'd gone for. Kingsley stood with his back to me, going through the contents of a bookcase on the other side of the cabin.

Clay was busy in the kitchen area, so it was to him I headed. He was the most easygoing out of the group, and I wanted to be around him to help me take my mind off whatever conversation Isaac might be having with their boss.

I approached him cooking eggs on the stove. "They're powdered." He apologized, as though it was his fault. "But it's the best we have."

"I'm sure they're fine." I gave him a tired smile. "What can I do to help?"

Clay frowned and leaned into me. He slipped his arm around my waist and pulled me closer, before dropping a kiss on top of my head. "You okay, sugar?"

I nodded. I put my arm around his waist, too, and returned the squeeze. "Yeah, of course. It's all just a bit overwhelming, you know?"

He glanced down at me, his stormy-gray eyes soft. "I don't know. This is the only kind of life I've ever known. It's always been danger and running, and thinking someone might turn around and shoot you at any moment. It's hard to imagine what a regular life would be like."

I moved away enough to give me space to twist to face him. "Jesus, Clay. That's no way to live."

"Isn't it?" He gave a lopsided grin. "What's the alternative? A dead-end job and spending every evening sitting on the couch drinking beer until you're dead?"

My lips twisted and I wrinkled my nose. "It's not that bad. You have to take pleasure in the little things, like your favorite dessert or a bright fall morning." Then I shook my head. "Hell, ignore me. I'm certainly not the right person to be giving anyone advice. It's not as though I've been skipping through life, enjoying every moment. My life's been pretty dark up until now."

"Up until now? So, you think this is better?"

I hesitated. "Maybe not the kidnapping part, or the getting shot at part, but I guess I'm getting used to having you guys around."

A voice came from behind me. "You're always so full of compliments, Darc."

I looked over my shoulder to see Alex behind me. He reached over the top of my head to open the cupboard and grab a glass, and, as he did so, his long, lean body pressed against the back of mine. I leaned out of the way to let him through. "What I mean to say is that you're not the kidnapping bastards I'd originally taken you for."

Clay chuckled. "There she goes again with the compliments."

I automatically smacked him with the back of my hand.

"So, what food have we got?" Alex peered into the pan and wrinkled his nose. "That looks like shit."

Clay stirred the eggs. "Yeah, well, we can't exactly order takeout all the way out here, so we have to make do. I found some bread in the freezer, so we'll toast it."

"It'll be fine," I said. "Thanks, Clay."

"There's coffee, too." He nodded to the pot brewing.

"Good. I need that more than the food."

"It won't be long," he replied. "I'll serve it all together."

Despite his complaints, Alex stepped in beside him. "I'll help."

I'd kicked Alex in the face the first time we'd met, and a part of me still felt a twinge of guilt about hurting him, though there was no way I could have known he was trying to help. Because that's what Alex did—he was born to help people.

I left Clay and Alex in the kitchen, and went to check on Lorcan. He lay on the couch, his eyes shut as I approached. I thought he was sleeping, and I turned to walk away again and leave him in peace, but he must have heard me because his eyes pinged open and locked with mine.

I gave him an awkward smile that was half an apology for waking him, and half me letting him know I was pleased to see him awake. "Sorry, didn't mean to wake you."

Lorcan swung his legs off the couch and pushed himself to sitting, grimacing as he did so, his hand covering his injured shoulder as though the pressure would help the pain. One of the other guys had found him a new t-shirt, so he no longer wore the bloodied one Alex had ripped in the back of the car on the way here.

"It's okay, you can stay lying down." I put out my hand to try to stop him moving any farther. I didn't want him putting himself in extra pain because of me.

"Nah, I'm fine." He patted the spot he'd freed up, and I slid onto the couch beside him. "I wanted to thank you for what you did in the car on the way here."

I frowned. "I didn't do anything. It was Alex who helped you."

He shook his head briefly and glanced away, as though he found what he was about to say difficult. "No, I meant about you holding my hand while he was doing it. It's stupid, I know, but we don't really hold hands with the other guys and having you do that helped take my mind off the pain."

Female comfort. That must be something they didn't get much of.

I gave a small smile. "I'm sure a girl's held your hand before."

He shrugged. "Not like that. Women have always been for one thing, you know? And in our line of work, it's not as though we can ever get attached. We never know where we're going to be from one moment to the next."

I arched my eyebrows. "You're saying women are for sex?"

"They know the score. We don't make any promises, because we can't keep them. It's one night, no attachments. Feelings never come into it. But when you were holding my hand in the car, it was different."

I nodded. "Yeah, it was."

I didn't tell him that his attitude—or even all their attitudes—to sex was exactly how I had been. They probably wanted me to be some little innocent, but that wasn't who I was at all. I'd been with men, and done exactly what they did. The moment anyone started to get attached, I was out of there so fast there was dust rising off my heels.

It had been different holding Lorcan's hand because I had felt something. I'd felt every time he'd winced in pain, and every second that passed since he was shot, I'd prayed he would be okay. Lorcan had been the first to kiss me, the one who'd instinctively seemed to know what I needed to bring me out of the hypnosis nightmare I'd found myself in. Before then, he'd seemed so distant, but now I thought he was just one of those people who watched and waited, and drank everything in, until the moment arrived where he needed to act.

"Anyway," he exhaled a breath, his head dropping down onto the back of the couch, "I'm glad you were there, that's all. I just wanted to say that. I wanted to say thanks."

He looked exhausted all over again, and his eyes slipped shut. I held back for a moment, and then impulsively leaned in and kissed Lorcan's cheek. His skin was rough from the dark stubble that poked through, and I resisted the urge to run my finger down the cleft in his chin. He opened one eye and side-glanced me, a hint of a smile tweaking his lips. I couldn't help smiling back, and a bubble of something swelled inside my chest. What was that feeling? It had been such a long time since I'd experienced it, it took me a moment to place. Happiness. Was I happy right in that moment, even though we'd been shot at, and the house had burned to the ground, and there was a good chance my Aunt Sarah was in danger? Yeah, here, with the guys, I felt good. Safe, and actually cared about. My aunt had always cared about me, but it was different with family. There was always a part of you that figured the only reason they cared was because you were bound by blood.

The guys had chosen to protect me.

Chapter Three

"Grub's up!" Clay called, plates slamming down onto the small kitchen table.

I got to my feet just as Alex brought Lorcan a plate so he could eat on the couch.

I looked at one of the empty spaces at the table. "Shouldn't we wait for Isaac?"

Clay wrinkled his nose. "Nah. He wouldn't expect us to wait. Depending on what sort of mood the boss is in, he could be awhile."

I slipped into one of the empty seats. Clay had served me up a portion exactly the same size as his own and the others, even though I was half the size of Kingsley. It wasn't an exciting meal, not like the Thai curry he'd cooked, but I hadn't eaten anything since being woken by the alarm back at the house, and that had been hours ago.

Though our circumstances were strange, I liked sitting around the table with all the guys. It made me feel like we were one big family. It had only ever been Aunt Sarah and me, sitting across from each other at the table, and before that it was only me and my dad. I'd never had lots of people around me, and, now that I did, I found I was starting to like it.

"Do you think he's going to be in a lot of trouble?" I asked, between shoveling forkfuls of egg into my mouth and taking bites of the crispy toast.

Kingsley looked across the table at me. "He's going to have some explaining to do, that's for sure. You can't torch a million-dollar house and not have something to say about it."

"Shit." My jubilant mood from a moment ago vanished. He'd had to blow up the house because of me, and I felt horrible that Isaac was now going to catch it in the neck because of something I'd done. Not only that, he wasn't even going to tell the truth and blame what had happened on me. I fought a sudden urge to jump to my feet and follow him down beneath the house and tell their boss it had all been my fault. But they'd said nothing good would come of that, so I remained fixed to my seat. My appetite had vanished, however, and I pushed my plate away.

"You not going to eat that?" Kingsley asked.

I shook my head, and he reached across to grab my plate and help himself to my leftovers.

Alex frowned at me. "You feeling okay?"

I nodded. "It just bothers me that Isaac is in trouble because of something I did."

Alex chuckled. "Don't feel bad for Isaac. He's a cold son of a bitch. Everything being said to him is probably rolling right off his back. Isaac never does anything he doesn't want to. If he's taking this on himself, it's because he wants to, not because he feels pressured into it."

I remembered how they'd all allowed me into the rest of the house and out of the cellar, even though Isaac had wanted to keep me down there, and I wondered how much of that was strictly true. But then I thought Isaac should have followed his first instinct and kept me locked up, and we'd still be in the big house instead of the cabin, and Lorcan wouldn't have been shot.

And you'd still be locked up in the cellar, and you wouldn't be eating meals around a table with a group of gorgeous, tough, dangerous men.

My thought was entirely selfish, but that didn't stop me thinking it. Would I rather be locked in the cellar right now, and for none of the events of that morning to have happened? No, I wouldn't, however horrible that made me sound.

The trap door in the middle of the floor swung open on its hinges—they hadn't replaced the rug or table, knowing Isaac was down there—and Isaac climbed out. He approached the table. His expression gave away nothing about what had happened down there.

"There's a plate warming in the oven." Clay jerked his head back toward the kitchen.

Isaac didn't make eye contact with me. "Thanks."

He went to the oven and opened the door, then used a tea towel to remove the plate. He carried the plate over and kicked out a chair, the legs scraping across the wooden floor, before setting the plate down, and sitting heavily on the chair. Without a word, he started to eat, and I couldn't take my eyes off him.

Nerves fluttered around in my stomach, but I forced myself to ask. "How did it go?"

He shrugged. "As expected." He alternated mouthfuls of egg with toast, and the bitter coffee, which had probably started to get cold by now.

"What's the next move?" Kingsley asked, scraping the final leftovers from the plate that had been mine, and then stacking it with his own empty plate.

Isaac glanced up from his food. "We're to stay here for the moment."

"Here?" I asked, looking around at the log walls. It was hardly a fortress. What would we do if Hollan found us and attacked? I didn't think there were any secret escape routes out of here, unless there was something hidden down in the cellar. "Are we going to be safe if we stay here?"

His head tilted to one side, regarding me. "We're as safe here as anywhere else, Darcy."

He hadn't really answered my question. Did that mean we weren't safe anywhere?

"And what about the memory stick and Hollan?"

Isaac nodded. "At least I was able to give him the good news that we have the code now. So, yes, Hollan and the memory stick is our next mission. Hollan won't keep the memory stick at FBI headquarters. He knows if anyone happened upon it, they'd automatically link your father's death, Darcy, with him. Hollan has a secret hideout of his own where we believe he'll have stashed the memory stick, but it's not as though he'll have it lying around in a drawer. I expect he'll have it locked away with a code of its own."

"So, we'd need to get Hollan in order to get that second code?" Alex said.

Isaac nodded. "Exactly. We can't just go in hoping to kill Hollan and grab the memory stick. If he's got it locked away somewhere, which he's bound to have, we're going to need to take him alive."

I balled my fists under the table, that familiar feeling of anger rumbling around inside of me. I didn't want Hollan to be taken alive. I wanted him dead, and I wanted to be the one to do it, but I knew saying so out loud to the guys wasn't going to get me anywhere. They might not take me along if they thought I'd do something to jeopardize their mission again.

"What about my Aunt Sarah?" I asked instead. "What did your boss say to do to help her?"

Isaac shook his head. He didn't quite meet my eye, his gaze flicking across me, not landing on my face. "He didn't. I'm sorry, Darcy. Your aunt isn't part of our project. We can't get her involved."

My stomach dropped. "But she might be in danger! You said so yourself."

"I know, but that's not our concern."

I brought my fists down hard on the table with a bang, making them all jump. "It's my concern! She's the only family I have left. I can't just abandon her." I forced myself to calm, inhaling through my nose, my jaw tight and lips pressed together as I thought hard. "You said before that Hollan was likely to be watching Aunt Sarah because he knew that would be my first point of contact, should I get the chance of contacting anyone, right?"

Isaac watched me, not giving anything away through his expression.

I rambled on. "He still wants me for the code, so is that idea of him watching Aunt Sarah going to change? If he wants me for the code, and you want him for the memory stick, isn't it a good idea to go to Aunt Sarah? It might lure him out enough for you to be able to take him captive."

Across the table, Kingsley sat up straighter, and Clay and Alex exchanged a glance.

"He'll still be proactive about trying to get to me for the code. He's not going to be just hanging out at this hideout of his, is he? Do you even know where it is?"

Lines appeared between Isaac's light brown eyebrows. "Not yet, but we'll find out."

"But only by finding Hollan," I said, warming to my theme, "and the best place to find him is probably my Aunt Sarah's house."

"She's got a point," Lorcan called out from the couch, and I delivered him a grateful smile.

Isaac fixed me with his green gaze, more curious now than annoyed. "So, you're suggesting we stake out your aunt's house and let Hollan come to us?"

"Exactly."

"If we do that," he said, "you're staying here."

I sat up straight, pushing my shoulders back and lifting my chin. "No chance. I'm the one Hollan wants." I wasn't going to let him sideline me. I had as much of a stake in this as any of them, if not more.

Isaac gave a frustrated growl. "That's why we can't risk him getting a hold of you."

"Unless I'm there, too, Hollan might not think it's even worth his while being there. He might just have his men deal with you guys. If they report back that I'm there, he's bound to come as well."

Isaac finished his food and got to his feet, shaking his head as he moved around the cabin. "I don't know. I don't like it."

"Neither do I, but if it works, then surely it's worth it."

His lips thinned, a muscle beside his eye twitching. "And if it doesn't, we lose you."

I took a breath. "Maybe that wouldn't be a bad thing either. You know Hollan wants the code and he's going to take me back to wherever he's got the memory stick hidden. You guys have the code now, and I'm sure as hell not telling Hollan. You just need to follow him, and he'll lead you right to it."

"With you as a hostage," he bit out.

My mouth ran dry. I could hardly believe I was suggesting such a thing. Had I completely lost my mind? I didn't want Hollan to grab me. I hated the bastard. But if it would help the others, then I'd do it for them. And I'd do it for my dad, too.

"He's not going to hurt me," I tried to reassure Isaac as much as myself. "He wants what's in my head."

Isaac stopped beside the sink and turned to face the table, his arms folded across his chest. "No, he's not going to kill you. But he can hurt you as much as he likes."

Silence fell around the table as what had just been discussed sank in.

"I don't like it," Clay said. "Maybe we can see if Hollan will come to the aunt's house, but I'm not going to offer up Darcy like some kind of reward package."

Alex shook his head. "I don't like it either. Going to her house is one thing, but I won't let Darcy be used like bait."

Kingsley rubbed his hand across his mouth. "I don't know. I think it's a good plan. If it was anyone other than Darcy..."

I jumped in. "Don't make me being a girl have anything to do with this decision. "If it was one of you guys, you wouldn't be thinking twice."

"If you were one of us," Kingsley said, "you'd have spent your life training for how to react in dangerous situations."

"Maybe. But my dad was an FBI agent, and I've not exactly led a sheltered life. I know how to take care of myself."

Isaac shook his head. "No, love. You're not going to offer yourself up to Hollan. But you can come with us to watch your aunt's house and see if Hollan goes there, okay? If he does, we can step in and grab him."

I knew his offer was to placate me, but I didn't want to push Isaac further. I was just relieved I'd be able to make sure Aunt Sarah was okay.

I nodded. "Agreed."

"There's no point in going today. Hollan will have lost men back at the house. He'll need to regroup, and refocus, too, and he'll expect us to do the same. We'll get some rest here, and leave in the early hours so we can get there under the cover of darkness."

"What about Lorcan?" I asked, wondering how he was going to cope with all this movement.

"I'll be all right," Lorcan called from the couch. "Some painkillers and a bit of rest and I'll be good as new."

"You were shot," I said in disbelief.

He rubbed his hand over the tattoos which vanished beneath the t-shirt sleeve hiding the bandaged wound. "Only a flesh wound. I'm fine."

These guys were tough, there was no doubt about that.

My pulse quickened at the thought of heading home again. Though it was the house I'd spent my whole life in, it felt as though it had been months since I'd last been there instead of a matter of days. I prayed Aunt Sarah would be okay. What was she thinking now, wondering what had happened to me? Did she believe me when I said I'd been taken, or did she still think I'd run off, or gotten myself involved with some illegal gang? She must have thought I was up to no good for the FBI to have gotten involved. I hoped she wasn't feeling disappointed in me. I longed to tell her the truth about what had been happening, but I certainly wasn't going to risk another phone call.

The next time I spoke to her, it would be face to face, and hopefully Isaac and the others would have Hollan and the location of the memory stick.

Chapter Four

Everyone had finished eating, so we rose from the table to help clean up. I learned Clay did the cooking, which meant he got out of the dishes. Seemed like a fair deal to me. Lorcan also got out of helping, on account of the gunshot wound, which also seemed fair.

I stood beside Kingsley as he washed up, his big hands sunk into the bowl, the white of the bubbles a contrast against his black skin. I used a tea towel to dry each plate as he handed it to me, the material squeaking against the clean surface. Kingsley teased me that I was doing a bad job and not drying things properly, bumping me with his hip, so I nudged him in return and pointed out any dirty spots he had missed.

"Darcy," Isaac called, interrupting us. "Got a minute? I want to show you something."

I glanced to Kingsley to make sure he didn't mind me abandoning my post, and he gave me a brief nod to tell me I could go. I finished the plate I'd been working on, stacked it in the cupboard, then walked over to where Isaac was waiting for me.

He watched me approach, his head doing that little tilting to one side thing he did. "I got the feeling you weren't overly convinced that we were well enough equipped here to be safe, so I wanted to put your mind at ease."

Isaac and I hadn't had the easiest of relationships so far, but that little bit of consideration caused something inside me to soften toward him. "Thanks, Isaac."

"You're welcome, love."

He went to the cellar trap door and swung it open, revealing the stairs leading down into darkness. As he did so, his shirt sleeve rode up a little, flashing the bandage which cover the cut I'd given him. My stomach turned at both the sight of the bandage and the hole in the ground.

I pulled a face. "Oh, God. Not the cellar!"

A horrible thought jarred through me. He wasn't going to lock me down there, was he? What if this was all just a lure, and the things he'd said at the table about me being allowed to come with them were all lies used to placate me?

No, I tried to reassure myself. The others wouldn't let him do that. They'd have my back. Yet the thought had made me realize I still didn't trust Isaac one hundred percent. Truth be told, he probably didn't fully trust me, either. After all, it had only been a few days earlier that I'd slashed his arm open with a razor blade.

Isaac chuckled, and I thought it might be the first time I'd ever heard him laugh. I didn't know what to think about the fact that the first thing that had made him laugh was also my discomfort.

"I won't lock you down there, I promise," he said, as though he'd plucked the thought from my head. He looked at me, his gaze intense, making my heart race. "I know you're not going anywhere."

I glanced back at the others, looking for reassurance. Lorcan napped on the couch. Alex had joined Kingsley at the sink. Clay was flicking through a book he had picked up, though I'd never taken him to be much of a reader. None of them appeared concerned about Isaac luring me into the cellar.

Isaac started down the steps, and, cautiously, I followed. He reached the bottom, and flicked on a switch. The room filled with light, and my mouth dropped open. The place was filled with computers, huge screens, and multiple keyboards. I remembered how one of the guys had told me computers were Isaac's thing. If that were the case, he must be in heaven down here.

"I wanted you to see that we're prepared. This place might not look like much, but it's kitted out should anything happen. The walls are coated in fire retardant paint, and so is the trap door leading down here. If something ever happened to the cabin, the whole place could burn to the ground, and everything sealed inside here would still be safe—including us, if needed."

I looked around at the innocuously white painted walls in surprise. They didn't look any different than any other painted wall. "That is reassuring."

I wondered if the cellar in the other house could have done with the same thing. They could have still burned the place down, but hidden down there and waited until Hollan and his men had gone. But then I remembered the amount of bricks and concrete that collapsed during the fire. This place was just a matter of logs and some furniture. We'd have had to have been dug out of the other cellar, and that still wouldn't have guaranteed survival. They'd done the right thing by running.

"Is this where you contacted your boss from?" I asked.

Isaac nodded. "Yeah, and I'm going to need to contact him again to let him know we plan to pin down Hollan at your house tomorrow. It would be best if you weren't down here when I did. What's happened with you—with us—isn't exactly protocol, and I don't want to give him any reason to think he needs to step in. Hollan finding us is bad enough. I don't want him to figure out the reason behind it."

"I'm sorry about—" I started, feeling wretched, but Isaac lifted a hand to cut me off.

"We learned from it," he said. "We all learned from it. Our treatment of you gave you every reason not to trust us, and we didn't trust you, either. I hope we can move past that now."

I nodded. "We can, thank you, Isaac." He was the one person I didn't think I'd ever thank. Yet strangely, after I'd allowed him to touch me in front of the others, a tenuous relationship had begun to build between us. I wondered if what happened would be a onetime thing, or if I'd ever get a repeat performance. He knew I'd kissed both Lorcan and Clay, though neither kisses had been intentional, they'd just kind of happened. I hadn't seen any kind of jealousy on any of the men's faces when Isaac had his fingers inside me. They'd watched, and I'd seen how their lips had parted, how they'd shifted positions, perhaps to hide erections, or even perhaps to apply more pressure where they'd wanted it, but none of them had told Isaac to stop.

"Leave me now," Isaac said, perhaps reading my thoughts on my face again. "I've got work to do." His persona had turned colder again. Maybe this was the man he needed to be for his work, but I thought there was a more passionate side of him underneath.

I did as he asked and turned and climbed back up the stairs. We'd left the hatch open when we'd come down, but after I'd climbed up, Clay stepped forward and swung the hatch back down again, shutting Isaac in.

"You're better off leaving him alone when he's working," Clay said.

"Yeah, that's what he told me. What's this boss of yours like? He seems scary."

"He's tough, but he has to be. Isaac makes some hard decisions, but this guy's decisions are a hundred times harder. He's the one who makes calls on things you won't have even thought to be a call."

I frowned, not understanding. "A call?"

"Some people aren't all they seem on the surface," he said cryptically. "Sometimes those people need to be taken out, for the good of the country."

My jaw dropped. "Are you talking about killing people?"

"They tend to be unfortunate accidents, but yes, sometimes people have to die."

The guys were killers? Sure, I'd seen them shoot the FBI agents who'd tried to take me from my home, but, looking back, I understood why they'd done it. If those men hadn't been killed, I'd be in Hollan's possession right now. Why did I think it was okay to justify those deaths to myself, but the idea of assassinating someone who was dangerous didn't sit right with me?

Isaac wasn't the only one good at reading my thoughts. "We're not the ones who are the assassins, sugar. I'm not saying we won't kill if we have to, but those jobs aren't given to us. I'm just trying to give you an idea of the sort of jobs our boss oversees."

I breathed a sigh of relief. I don't know why it was important for me not to see them as some kind of undercover assassin team, but it was.

Alex had taken a seat beside Lorcan on the couch and was working on changing the dressing. Blood had soaked through the first, but it appeared to have stopped now. When Alex wiped down the wound, Lorcan didn't wince as badly as he'd done during the application of the first dressing in the car. I hated to think of what might have happened if the bullet had landed just a little farther to left. If it had hit his spinal cord, or had even ended up more deeply embedded in his shoulder, Lorcan could have died. This place would have a whole different feel to it if Lorcan had died in the house or back in the car. I couldn't imagine one of the guys missing, yet tomorrow we'd be putting ourselves in danger once again, and there was always a chance someone might not make it back.

I left them to it, and went to explore the rest of the cabin.

I discovered three bedrooms, two with two single beds each, and the third with a double. I didn't need to be good at math to figure out there were six of us and five beds, which meant I'd be sharing with someone again. I'd be happy to share with any of them except Isaac. Despite the fact he'd had his fingers inside me, I still found him the most intimidating, and I didn't think I'd stand any chance of sleeping if he was lying beside me.

Lorcan, with his shoulder, also needed some space.

When I went back into the living area, Isaac was climbing back out of the cellar.

"Okay, we're good to go," he said, swinging the hatch back down. This time, he pulled the rug across it, too, and Clay stepped in to help.

With the furniture back in place, Isaac straightened. "I want us to be prepared. Each room has a gun safe, and we can take extra weapons from them for tomorrow. I'm sure we'll be fine for tonight, but, in case we need it, the code on each of them is six-one-nine-one." He looked toward me. "Think you can remember that?"

The numbers jumped in front of my eyes, flashing over again in order. Six-one-nine-one.

They still didn't know about my synesthesia. "Yeah, I think I'll be able to remember that."

"Good. We still have the guns we took from the house, and there's spare ammo in the cabinet above the refrigerator. I'm not expecting any trouble here, but it's always best to be prepared."

"Were you a Boy Scout, too?" I asked with a grin.

His gaze was cool, not returning my smile. "We're better than Boy Scouts."

I looked around. "So, where's everyone going to be sleeping?"

Clay stepped in beside me and possessively hooked his arm around my neck. "Alex got you last night. Tonight, you're all mine."

His words sent a thrill through me and I glanced up at him. He gave me a wink. The memory of our little make out session at the top of the stairs was fresh in my mind, and a shiver of anticipation went through me at the thought of being in such close proximity to Clay all night.

Someone could have offered to take the couch, but I didn't want that, and, from the lack of offers, I knew they didn't either.

"Behave yourself, Clay," Isaac warned.

"Aww." He gave a mock pout. "Now, where is the fun in that?"

I trapped a smile between my lips, though the tugging at my cheeks gave my true feelings away. I didn't think Clay had any intention of behaving himself.

"Okay, everyone," Isaac said. "It's about four hours' drive to D.C., so we need to leave here by one a.m. to get there before it's fully daylight, and take up position where we can't be seen. Darcy, I'm hoping you can give us some ideas about the best spots to watch the house from."

I nodded. "Sure."

"Try to get a few hours' sleep, everyone. We're going to need to be as alert as possible for tomorrow."

It was still early—barely after eight p.m.—but the day had been crazy, and I was beat.

The guys let me use the bathroom first. I found some still-wrapped toothbrushes in the medicine cabinet, so I was at least able to brush my teeth. I guessed I'd just sleep in Alex's t-shirt again, though I was going to need a change of clothes at some point. I reminded myself we'd be back at my house at the break of dawn tomorrow. If all went well, I'd be able to grab a change of my own clothes. The idea of putting on my own bra and underwear again was a ridiculous thing to look forward to, but I was.

I finished up and slipped out of the bathroom to let Kingsley in after me.

He dipped his head at me as he passed. "Good night, Darcy."

"Night, Kingsley."

His dark gaze slipped down my body to my naked legs and back up again.

His massive body blocked the doorway to the bathroom for a moment, and then the door shut behind him. Voices of some of the others, still hanging out in the kitchen, filtered through to me, but I left them to it and went straight to the room with the double bed.

Chapter Five

I slipped between the sheets of the double bed and tried not to think about who might have lain here before me. It was barely dark outside, but I'd drawn the curtains before climbing in, wanting to shut out any remaining light so I could sleep. I also wanted to block out the sight of the forest beyond, my imagination turning the twisted branches of the trees into monstrous arms reaching out to snatch me from my bed.

I didn't have to wait long before the bedroom door opened and Clay walked in. Twisting, I glanced over my shoulder at him. He was utterly unselfconscious as he flipped open the buckle of his jeans, popped the button and let the jeans fall from his narrow hips. Then he tugged off his t-shirt and threw it to the floor to join the jeans. I guessed Clay wasn't exactly a neat-freak, but my mind wasn't on his tidiness. Instead, my gaze raked across the perfection of his body—the spatter of blond hair across the curve of his pectorals vanished as it reached the squared bricks of his abdominals.

He looked toward me on the bed, and I quickly turned back around, hoping he hadn't noticed me watching him.

The bed dipped with his weight as he climbed in the other side. The bed covers lifted, wafting across my body, allowing cool air to touch my skin. My flesh puckered in goose bumps, and I shivered.

"You're cold." Clay slid in closer, and the blankets settled down around us.

"A little," I admitted.

Clay's arm hooked around my waist, and he pressed his face against my shoulder, spooning me. "Tell me why you smell like Alex," he said, his tone teasing.

I wriggled away, creating some space between us. "Because I'm wearing his t-shirt."

"Damn, girl. You need to take that off and put mine on instead."

I laughed. "No, I don't. I'm comfortable as I am."

Clay exhaled a sigh. "I guess I can live with you smelling like Alex. If I have to share to keep you around, then that's what I'll do."

I twisted to face him. "Share? Is that what's going on here?"

His eyes locked with mine, tumultuous thunderclouds passing across them. He pushed a hand through his hair. "What do you think is going on here, Darcy? You let Isaac touch you that way in front of us all, you kissed me before, and we all saw you kissing Lorcan."

"That was different," I said, but my voice was barely above a whisper. The thought of being able to have all the guys made my nipples harden into pebbles, and a familiar tightening swirled at my core. It had occurred to me, hadn't it? The idea of being passed around between them. When I'd been held down in the cellar, I'd even thought about how it would happen—one at a time, or with all their hands and mouths and cocks on me at once. The thought caused heat to pool between my thighs, my clit tingling with arousal.

Clay was here, now, so close. I had a desire I needed to sate, and he was one very willing man. I could push him away, and tell him no, and I knew he would listen, but what would I be doing it for? The guys had all watched Isaac finger me, while I stood compliant, so who would I be trying to impress? Would it just be that I was trying to stand up to some moral code that I didn't even care about? I didn't belong to any one of these men individually. I belonged to all of them, and right now it was Clay here, and he wanted me.

My lips parted, my tongue flicking out to wet them. Clay watched my mouth and then lifted his hand to place a finger on my lower lip. I went with it, allowing my tongue to snake out again and touch his finger with the tip. His breathing grew ragged, and though there was still space between us, I felt sure I could put my hand down the front of his body and find his cock, erect and begging for attention.

"Ah, fuck, sugar," he growled. "You have no idea how much I want that pretty mouth of yours."

His words made me hotter, and, without thinking any further, our bodies crashed together. Clay's mouth crushed to mine, and I parted my lips, wanting him as badly as he wanted me. The kiss was a little too hard, stealing my breath, possessive, claiming me. Then his tongue was in my mouth, and I kissed him back with equal fervor, both of us hungry for each other. Every synapse fired within me, and I let out an involuntary moan, pressing my body up harder against him. Clay's hands reached up the shirt I was wearing—Alex's shirt—and his fingers found one of my breasts, pinching and rolling the nipple. The sensations made me gasp, firing sparks down directly between my legs, and I arched my back to push my breast deeper into his grasp.

I slid my hand down the front of his body and discovered the bulge in his shorts I'd predicted. I wanted to touch him, to feel him, to give him the same pleasure he was giving me. After all, we could all be dead tomorrow, and then I'd regret not making the most of this now.

He kissed down my neck, and his long hair tickled my skin. "Can I get rid of the t-shirt now?"

I giggled. "Okay, but don't tell Alex."

"Don't worry. I'll make sure you're wearing one of mine next time you bunk up with him."

I almost laughed again, but Clay's mouth around my nipple stopped me in my tracks, and I let out a moan instead. I reached for his cock and slipped inside the front of his shorts, my fingers meeting with silky skin, hardness, and heat. I closed my fingers around him, and he let out a groan, the sound sending vibrations through the sensitive flesh of my areola. I moved my hand up and down his length, pumping him slowly as he bucked his hips into my palm.

His hand moved between my thighs, pushing inside my panties, stroking me, so differently to how Isaac had done. Isaac had been firm and hard, as though he'd had a job to do, and he wouldn't let anyone distract him from doing it, but Clay's touch was slow and sweet. His finger caressed over the nub of my clit, making me gasp as electricity fired through my core. My hold on his cock tightened and I increased my momentum, and in return his hand moved lower, parting my swollen, wet folds, and then pushing up inside me.

Two different men had put their fingers inside me in less than twelve hours. I was no innocent angel, but it felt insane. And the strangest part of it was that I didn't feel any of the guilt I'd been expecting. I didn't belong to any one of the guys more than the other; this was just how it was when we were together.

Clay hooked his finger inside my channel, feeling for the little bundle of nerves that would send me to a whole other level. My hips rocked against his hand, and my arousal built in a steady coil, rising from between my thighs and threatening to crash all through my body.

His other hand moved from my breast to my hair, his fingers knotting as we kissed again, hurried and urgent, bites and licks, and hot breath on our faces.

"Fuck, I want to be inside you, sugar. I want to know how it feels to have your pussy clamped around my dick as hard as it's clamping around my fingers right now."

"Yes," I gasped between hurried kisses. "I want you, too."

His fingers slipped from my body, and I could smell myself on the air.

"Wait, we haven't got anything," I said.

"What?" He looked up at me from beneath his curtain of hair.

"You know, to be *safe*." I lifted my eyebrows to make my point.

"Shit."

He rolled out of bed, and then half-hopped, one leg half-in and half out of his shorts, his very firm backside on display. I cupped my hand over my mouth to hold back my laughter as he made it to the door and peered out to make sure he wasn't going to be caught by any of the others.

Clay vanished out the door, and I stayed propped up on my elbow anticipating his return. I hoped there would be some condoms in the bathroom. This place was pretty well stocked, but if whoever did the stocking expected only the guys to be here, we might be out of luck.

But within less than a minute, he sauntered back in, looking at me as though I was a rib eye steak, and dangling a strip of foil packets from one hand. He wiggled his eyebrows. "Looks like someone anticipated us getting busy."

I grinned.

He shucked off his shorts, leaving him standing there in all his beautiful nakedness. His skin looked about glued to the hollows of his abs, his navel a perfect circle with a trail of hair that led down to the promise of what was to come. I reached for him, and he climbed back onto the bed. Clay hadn't lost any of his erection during the quick trip to get the condoms, and he sat back on his heels. He tore off the top of the packet, and I moved closer, crawling up to him. Before he got the chance to put the condom on, I leaned into his lap and closed my mouth around the head of his cock. He sucked air in over his teeth, as though he were in pain, and then his hand settled in my hair. I circled his dick with my lips and bobbed lower and then back up again, tasting the salt of his pre-cum.

His voice came ragged above me. "Baby-doll, as much as I love you doing that to me, I'm going to shoot my load down the back of your throat any minute now, if you keep that up, and I sure as hell didn't get those condoms for nothing."

I looked up at him, how he was looking down at me, his blond locks hanging in his face, his eyes turbulent with arousal, his lips slack with lust. I gave him a look that tried to be all innocent—*who me?*—fluttering my eyelashes while I still had my lips wrapped around his cock.

But I released him from my mouth, and the moment I did so, he rolled the protection down his length, and then pushed me back on the bed. He moved between my thighs, and I spread them wide for him and then wrapped my legs around his body, hooking my heels into the hard muscle of his ass. It only took the slightest nudge, and his cock pushed inside me, stretching me. I cried out, bucking up against him.

"Shh, sugar. You're gonna wake the whole house up." He placed his hand over my mouth, and I parted my lips, tasting his fingers and my arousal on his skin. With his other hand, he grabbed one wrist and then managed to snatch the other, and held them both above my head. He held me pinned to the bed, one hand covering my mouth to stifle my cries, the other holding my arms so I couldn't move. The position flipped my mind back to how we'd first met, how I'd been held captive by the men, and how I'd believed this would be my fate. It shot an uneasy spurt of adrenaline through me, putting my body on high alert. It was different now, though—this wasn't against my will, even if he held me as though it was.

He fucked me, slamming into me, not fast but with slow, deliberate movements, pushing hard and deep so I felt him filling the whole of me, and then pulling back out almost to the point of slipping from my body, before driving back home.

The sex wasn't only about physical release. It was also a life affirmation after what we'd been through that day, and a way of forgetting what we still had to come.

And as my orgasm took hold, making my toes curl, my breath gripped behind clenched teeth, I didn't think of anything except the man losing himself inside me.

Chapter Six

"Time to wake up, guys."

Kingsley was at the bedroom door, already dressed. He was wearing different clothes from the ones he'd been wearing yesterday—a shirt and jeans combo that looked great on him. I guessed there must be changes of clothing for the guys in the other bedrooms.

He looked between Clay and me, but didn't comment on the way we were tangled together, my head resting on Clay's chest, my leg hooked over his thigh. Thankfully, I'd managed to put Alex's t-shirt back on before falling asleep, so at least he hadn't found us naked.

I sat up and rubbed my eyes, and Clay stirred beside me.

"Ugh," I groaned. "Waking up at this time is not natural."

Kingsley smiled affectionately at my reaction, flashing his white teeth. "Alex is making coffee. I'll have a cup waiting for you when you get out."

"That would be awesome. Thanks, Kingsley."

He turned from the doorway and left us to it.

Knowing I needed to get straight up or else I'd end up falling back to sleep again, I climbed out of bed, shivering against the chill of the night air. I went to the window and pulled back the curtains. Outside, the black silhouettes of branches waved across a night sky speckled with stars. There was no light pollution out here, and the stars stretched on forever. It felt like the middle of the night, because it *was* the middle of the night. We were driving back to my home today.

The thought made my stomach churn with nerves. I wanted to see my house again, and most of all, I wanted to see Aunt Sarah safe and well, and to let her know I was okay, too, but it was who might be waiting for us that had me worried.

"Have I got five minutes to grab a shower?" I asked Clay, twisting to look over my shoulder to where he was still sitting up in bed, the sheets wrapped around his narrow waist. "I need to wake myself up." That and I could smell sex clinging to my skin. I wasn't ashamed or embarrassed about spending the night with Clay, but I didn't want the others to be quite so viscerally aware of it.

A yawn crawled its way up my throat, and I put the back of my hand over my mouth, trying to hold it in.

"Could do with a few more hours myself," Clay said, noticing my yawn.

He hopped out of bed and yanked his jeans back on. As he looked down to button them up, his blond locks fell over his face, and I took a moment to appreciate the outline of muscles of his abdominals and the little line of hair that disappeared into the waistband of his shorts. *I know exactly where that trail leads*, I thought with a secret inner smile.

He glanced up at me through his hair and grinned. "The look on your face right now is absolutely filthy."

My teeth grazed my lower lip as I held back an even filthier smile.

"Damn, girl. If we didn't have to get out of here soon, I'd—"

The door pushed open, cutting off his words, and Alex stuck his head through the gap. "Coffee's ready. We've got to get a move on."

He vanished again, the door swinging shut behind him.

I remembered my need for that shower. I picked up my clothes, knowing they were dirty, but not having anything to change into. They would have to do. Hopefully, I'd be able to grab something from my house at some point today, assuming all went well.

I didn't know what kind of direction I expected today to take. If I thought I was just going to be able to walk back into my home and start picking out my wardrobe, I was probably kidding myself. Things were almost certainly not going to run that smoothly, but I didn't want to consider the possibility of them not going our way.

I left Clay in the bedroom and headed out to the bathroom. I'd half expected to bump into one of the other guys coming out, but it seemed everyone was already up and ready to go. They were clearly more used to activity in the middle of the night than I was. I still felt half asleep, and deep down I wanted nothing more than to curl up back under the covers and sleep for another five or six hours. But that luxury wasn't going to happen, and I didn't want the men to think I was holding them back in any way. Just taking the five minutes to shower was probably delaying them.

In the bathroom, I turned on the shower and waited until it ran hot. Quickly, I stripped off Alex's t-shirt and the underwear I'd slipped back on, and then jumped underneath the flow of water. My body had that sensitive, slightly swollen, just-fucked feeling, and I squirmed as I found some soap and ran my hands over my skin. A part of me had been waiting for that to happen with Clay. My thoughts went to the others. Would they treat me differently now? Would I be off limits? I didn't think so—after all, Isaac had put his claim on me before Clay had, and that hadn't stopped what we'd done last night.

The thought of getting intimate with each of the guys excited me, and if I hadn't known we'd been pressed for time, I'd have allowed my hand to slip between my thighs and let my imagination run wild. But they were waiting for me, and it was important I didn't become a liability to them.

I switched off the water and towel dried, and then put my t-shirt on. I wrinkled my nose at my dirty panties, and decided to forgo them altogether. My jeans were enough to cover my ass, and so I stashed the dirty underwear in my pocket instead.

Feeling cleaner and more awake, I headed out into the kitchen to find all five of the men waiting for me.

"There she is." Alex handed me a mug of now cooling coffee. "It should be fine to drink."

"Thanks." I accepted the caffeine gratefully.

I caught Clay's eye, and we exchanged a small smile I hoped no one else analyzed too deeply.

I spotted dark hair and a leather jacket. "Hey, Lorcan. How are you feeling?"

Lorcan touched his shoulder. "I'm okay. Just as long as I don't get shot again today, right?"

I frowned at him in disapproval. "Don't even joke about it."

He threw me a wink to tell me he was kidding, and I narrowed my eyes and pulled a face at him.

Isaac hadn't acknowledged my arrival, working on a small laptop I assumed he'd taken from the stash of equipment downstairs. On the kitchen table lay multiple guns of various sizes, and beside each one sat spare clips of ammunition. It looked like we were going to war, and I swallowed hard at the sight of them. Memories from being shot at the previous day were still fresh in my mind, and, as much as I didn't want to get shot myself, it was the thought of one of the guys getting hurt that worried me the most. What if it wasn't just a flesh wound next time? What if one of them was seriously injured or worse? I wished there was another way around getting hold of the memory stick, but this was their job. Me trying to convince them not to do it would fall on deaf ears, and besides, I was invested in this, too. I wanted to see Hollan dead, and I wanted to know what information would be unlocked by the code my father had given me.

Was this something I could just walk away from? I didn't think so. Until Hollan was dead, I wouldn't be safe. And we didn't even know if it would end with Hollan. For all we knew, someone else might be working above him, and taking out Hollan would only mean that someone else would step into his place.

"You okay, Darcy?" Kingsley frowned at me. He must have picked up on my silence.

I nodded. "Yeah, just thinking about today."

Isaac finally looked up from what he was doing. "You don't have to come. It would probably be safer for us all if you didn't." He'd gone back into cold fish mode, and I was starting to recognize that this was working Isaac. I thought he had another layer to him, one that was kinder, and did care, but in his line of work it seemed he had no room for feelings or sentimentality.

I shook my head. "No, it's fine. You might need me to lure Hollan out."

Isaac scowled. "I don't like that idea."

I skipped over the possibility in case Isaac changed his mind. It would be even worse to be left here alone, knowing the others were going to my house and putting themselves in danger. What I'd be imagining would probably be far worse than the reality. "Anyway, I really need to see Aunt Sarah. She must be out of her mind with worry about me."

"You might not get the chance to speak to her directly," Isaac warned, fixing me with his green eyes, his expression serious. "If she's surrounded by Hollan's men, it'll be too dangerous for you to go in there."

I nodded. "I know."

He pointed a finger at me. "And no doing anything reckless, okay? You remember what happened last time."

He was talking about the phone call I made, exposing our location to Hollan, and heat torched my face. I twisted my fingers in the strands of my hair and glanced down at the floor, not wanting to make eye contact with anyone. "Yeah, I remember."

"Good."

Someone shoved a packet under my nose, forcing me to look up. Clay gave me a lopsided smile. "Pop-Tart?"

I wrinkled my nose. "I think I'll pass, but thanks. It's a bit early for me to stomach food yet." He'd broken the tense moment with Isaac, and I was thankful to him for that.

"Okay." Kingsley got to his feet. "Let's pack up and ship out."

That was our cue to move. Each of the men went to the table, selecting their weapon of choice and the spare ammo to go with it. I was left with the same gun I'd been given the previous day. That they trusted me enough to make sure I was armed made me feel better. Yes, I'd messed up, but I'd also been able to give them vitally important information, and I needed to remember that. I had a part in all of this. If they didn't have me, they'd never stand a chance pulling whatever information was on the memory stick, should they ever get hold of it. Of course, they still hadn't trusted me enough to tell me what was on it yet. I hoped I wasn't helping them get access to something that would see a whole heap of people hurt.

I made a mental note to ask them again, but I wasn't going to do it right now. I didn't want to give them any reason to be annoyed with me and leave me behind. Besides, I had to remember my dad had taken the flash drive initially, and he'd been the one to give me the code. He wouldn't have done that if he'd thought what was on it would hurt people, would he?

The men had started to pile out to the vehicles waiting outside. I made sure the safety was on, then tucked the gun into the waistband at the back of my jeans. I'd never been a fan of the things, especially after my dad was shot, but right now, knowing I had a way of defending myself, made me feel safer.

Having five young, heavily armed men surrounding me also didn't hurt.

"We'll take both cars," said Isaac. "Darcy, you're in with me, Kingsley, and Lorcan. Alex and Clay, you follow behind."

I experienced a dip of disappointment at not getting to be in the car with Alex and Clay. I'd have swapped Isaac for either of them in a heartbeat, but I suspected Isaac knew that. He probably didn't want either me or the guys to get too emotionally involved. It might cloud our judgment went when we needed to remain clearheaded.

Outside, the cold fresh air hit my lungs, making me inhale sharply. The night sky was clear, stars winking down at us. I wrapped my arms around my body, protection against the chill. I was looking forward to getting the heat going once we were on the road. Somewhere in the distance came the haunting hoot of an owl. I jumped at the crack of twigs in the depths of the forest surrounding us, signifying a nocturnal mammal going about its business, perhaps interested in the activity of the not-so-nocturnal mammals busying themselves around the cars.

Kingsley got behind the wheel, and Isaac took the passenger seat. He still held the small laptop in his lap, and I wondered what he was doing on it. Communicating with the people he worked for, perhaps?

I slid into the back seat, and Lorcan got in beside me.

"Hey," he said, giving me a nod.

"Hey, yourself."

I shivered again, violent shudders across my shoulders. It was partly from the cold, but also from tension, and fear of what the very early start to this new day would hold.

"Crank up the heat, will you, Kingsley?" Lorcan called out to the front. "Our princess is cold."

I smacked him on the thigh. "I'm no princess."

He held my gaze in the moonlight streaming through the back window. "That's good, 'cause we're no knights in shining armor either."

Lorcan looked at me just a little too long, and my cheeks heated, forcing me to be the first to glance away.

The car got moving, headlights illuminating the forest around us. It was strange how something that appeared so tranquil and beautiful in the daytime became full of haunting and mystery in the night. The headlights of our car, and the vehicle containing Clay and Alex following, swept across the swathe of trees and the dirt track beyond. I wondered if something could have been hiding there, watching us, and the thought sent another shiver down my spine.

Lorcan must have noticed again. He thumped the back of the seat in front. "Where's that heat?"

"It's coming, man," said Kingsley. "Chill out."

"We are chilled, that's the problem."

Seconds later, hot air blasted at us through the vents, and I began to thaw. Though I'd done my best not to get my hair wet in the shower, the ends, and at the nape of my neck, had gotten damp, and that hadn't helped when I'd hit the cold outside air.

With nothing else to do, I sat back in my seat and stared out of the window. I put my hand to my mouth and chewed anxiously at the dry skin surrounding my nails. I wished I had my phone with me—this would be the perfect time to distract myself on social media with videos of cats and photographs of other people's food. It would help take my mind off what was going to happen when morning broke.

The interior of the car started to warm up, but I still couldn't relax. It was the middle of the night, and I probably could have done with sleeping another few hours, but the caffeine from the coffee was working its way around my system.

"Bingo," Isaac said from the passenger seat.

I perked up, relieved to have something to distract me from my thoughts. "What is it?"

"I've got visual on the house."

"What house?"

He twisted in his seat to look back at me. "Your house. It's dark, so I can't make out too much right now, but as soon as it starts getting light, we should be able to see if there's anyone suspicious lurking around."

I sat forward. "Can I see?"

Isaac lifted the laptop so I could see the screen. I'd been hoping to see my home, but all it showed was a few dark shapes and some specks of light from the street lamps and a couple of security lights. I wrinkled my nose in disappointment.

"We'll be there in a few hours," said Lorcan, picking up on how I felt.

I gave him a grateful smile. "Yeah, but I don't know what to hope for—that Hollan is there and we're able to find the memory stick and make him pay for what he did, or to hope we don't find anyone, and I'm able to go home and give my aunt a hug, and get a fresh change of clothes." I gave a small laugh at how stupidly opposite the two possible situations were. Gun fights and abduction, or hugs and clean clothes.

Sadness swelled inside me, making my eyes prick with tears and my throat tighten in a knot.

How had my life ended up in this place?

I knew how. My father telling me that code.

Had he realized he was making me a target when he told me? Or had his actions been done in panic, knowing the code would die with him if he didn't? I hoped it was the second option. Thinking he'd potentially signed my death warrant with his final breath caused my insides to twist, making me nauseated.

Fingertips lightly brushed the back of my hand, and I looked over to see Lorcan frowning at me in concern. I glanced down to where our hands touched. Lorcan's fingers were long, the nails squared, and I briefly wondered if he might play an instrument—the piano, or perhaps guitar would be more suited to him.

"You okay?" He kept his voice low. "You look upset."

I sniffed and nodded. "Yeah, just thinking about my dad."

"I'm sure he never meant for all of this to happen." He gave me a smile that was supposed to be reassuring but didn't quite get past rueful.

"I'm trying to convince myself of that."

His fingers slipped around the back of my hand and solidified into a firmer hold. I smiled at him gratefully. I could see he was trying to offer me the same comfort as I'd tried to give him yesterday. It was a different type of pain—mine emotional as opposed to the very physical agony he'd gone through—but often physical pain heals far more quickly than an emotional one, especially when the person who'd caused the pain was no longer around to get closure from.

We sat like that, just holding hands, and though it was such a simple thing, it helped me feel better.

Chapter Seven

As the vehicle ate the miles, bringing us closer to the city, my anxiety increased. I continued to check out of the rear window, making sure Clay and Alex were still with us, and that no one else looked like they were following.

After a couple of hours, the sky began to fade from pitch black to a deep, cobalt blue. One by one, the stars winked out, as though they were flames extinguished by the hand of God. In the front seat, Isaac folded open his laptop again, and I knew what he was doing.

I leaned over the back of the seat, pulling the seat belt loose so I had room. "Are you able to see anything yet?"

He was looking at an aerial view of my street. With the burgeoning light, I was able to make out our back yard and the chimney on the roof of our house.

Isaac nodded. "Getting there. Another hour or so, and I'll be able to spot if anyone is on lookout on the street, or if any of the vehicles appear suspicious."

"How are you going to be able to tell a suspicious vehicle from a non-suspicious one?"

"If one is doing loops of the area, they'll be easy enough to pick out. And if there's a car you don't recognize parked opposite the house, we'll keep an eye on that as well. At this time of day, a lot of people will be driving to work, so the residential streets should clear out of traffic fairly quickly. It'll make the ones who aren't supposed to be there more noticeable."

I stared at the screen, trying to spot anything that didn't seem right. But it wasn't light enough yet, and the cars only appeared to be dark shapes dotted around the streets.

"What if Hollan is already inside?" I asked. "How will we know?"

"He won't be inside without anyone else around to watch out for him. He'd leave himself open to us surrounding him, and he's too smart to do that."

I nodded. "Makes sense. What if he's not there at all?"

"Then you go and see your aunt, and we'll figure out what to do next. But whatever happens, we need to find Hollan. Now we have the code, we need the memory stick. One is no good without the other, and, as far as we know, Hollan is the only one who knows where the damned thing is."

"And as far as he knows, I'm the only one who knows the code."

Isaac nodded. "True. He doesn't know you've told us."

His teeth dug into his lower lip as he thought. I wondered what was going through his head. Isaac seemed to have one of those minds that was always thinking and plotting. I wondered if he ever just sat back and relaxed. I doubted it.

Isaac snapped the lid of the laptop down again, signaling our conversation was over.

I sat back and leaned the side of my head against the window. We'd been in the car for almost three hours, and everyone was starting to get uncomfortable, shifting in their seats. The guys, with their long legs, must have found the cramped space worse.

"Right, guys," Kingsley said from the driver's seat. "I'm gonna go cross-eyed if I have to stare at the road much longer."

Isaac looked back at Lorcan and me. "Let's take a comfort break. It'll be better for us to be refreshed if we need to deal with Hollan and his men when we reach Darcy's house."

We pulled over at the next truck stop we came across and climbed out with groans of relief, stretching stiff arms, legs, and backs. Clay and

Alex had pulled over with us, and they both got out, too. I tried not to stare too hard when Clay lifted his hands above his head in a stretch, revealing a flash of hard abs.

"Who wants more coffee?" Alex glanced at the truck stop cafe.

Everyone's hands rose into the air.

"Can I grab a bottle of water, too?" I felt bad for being awkward, but I was dehydrated, and though I needed the caffeine from the coffee, the beverage wouldn't help with my thirst.

Alex nodded. "Of course. You want to give me a hand?"

I shrugged. "Sure."

Everyone needed bathroom stops, and my own bladder needed emptying, but I figured I'd help Alex get the coffees first, and then I'd take my turn. I followed his tall, lean back into the service station. The lights were on inside, and the shapes of people were silhouetted at the window. At this time in the morning, the place was filled with truckers, and, other than a couple of older women who looked like they were either truckers' wives, or truckers themselves, I was the only female below the age of fifty. Alex also stood out among the small crowd. He looked far too clean cut, and had the air of someone who'd studied well beyond leaving high school. But he was also well over six feet tall, and the sharpness of his blue eyes and the jut of his jaw also made him look like someone you wouldn't want to mess with.

I stuck close to his side as we went to the counter.

Glancing over my shoulder, I found several pairs of male eyes lingering on me. I received a salacious grin as I accidentally caught the eye of one of the men. Ugh. He must have been at least forty, with a gut that pressed a fold of flab into the edge of the table. He gave me a wink, and I looked away. I didn't want to give him the idea I was interested. If the guy had been here alone, I'd have told him to fuck off, but he had a number of his buddies with him, all with the unhealthy pallor of someone who spent too much time sitting down, eating fast food, and not getting regular hours of sleep. It was best just to ignore men like that. They'd never change, no matter what clever retort you came up with.

"I wanted to see how you were getting on," Alex said, after he'd ordered six black coffees and a bottle of water for me. There was no messing around with skinny Frappuccinos with extra foam with these guys.

"I'm okay. I guess I just want this to be over with."

I did, but I didn't. Again, I was back to the thought of what would happen to me after this was all done with. Once Isaac and the others got the memory stick back, and were able to access the information on it, would I just be sent home to continue living my pointless life? If Hollan was dealt with, I wouldn't be in danger anymore. The thought of them all leaving me caused pain to tighten in my chest. It had barely been a week since they'd all burst so dramatically into my life, yet now I struggled to picture myself going back to my old life. Would I continue to search for crappy jobs I didn't want? Would I work on improving my relationship with Aunt Sarah? Hell, maybe I would even get myself a proper boyfriend, though after having the five of them in my life, whoever came along next would have a lot to live up to.

Was this the reason I'd never bothered to get emotionally involved with a guy? I'd had plenty of men I'd messed around with, but the moment any of them gave the slightest hint at being interested in anything other than what was in my panties, I'd run a mile. Had, deep down, I known I'd never be able to get everything I needed from just one man? Had some part of me known I'd end up frustrated at all the things they wouldn't be able to provide me with, either physically or emotionally, and that I would have just gotten bored, so we'd have ended up in one big mess? With each of these guys, I didn't feel there was a chance I'd ever end up bored or unsatisfied. They each took care of me in their own way, and they never made me feel I should be with one of them more than the other. Whatever mood I was in, they each picked up on which of them fitted best with me at that time. Would there ever come a time where I'd have them all together? I couldn't imagine that—five gorgeous men, each with their hands and mouths on me. It was the kind of thing only fantasies were made from, and yet here I was, with the very real possibility of it hanging in my future. I didn't want to mess this up.

Alex's voice yanked me from my fantasy. "Sure, I understand." He paid the cashier for the drinks, then twisted to face me. "I don't want to speak out of turn, but remember I'm a medical doctor, so if you need anything ... medical ... just give me a shout."

I stared at him for a moment, trying to figure out what he was talking about. Then it dawned on me that Alex and Clay had just spent several hours alone in the car together. Had Clay told him about what we'd done the previous night? Had it been like boy-talk, discussing the details, ribbing each other about what I was like in bed?

My cheeks flared with heat. Medical stuff. Did he mean birth control? Oh, my God. I just about wanted to die.

"I'm fine," I said, my tone curt. This wasn't a conversation I wanted to have with him. It made me feel as though he was trying to be some concerned big brother, or even my dad, and the whole thing made me feel icky. That wasn't how I thought about Alex at all, and I hated the idea of him and Clay talking about me in that way.

The clerk placed a couple of coffee cups on the counter, and I grabbed them to take them back out to the others, wanting to be out of there. I shoved open the door of the café with my shoulder, ignoring the stares from the truckers, and stormed back to where the rest of the guys were waiting. I couldn't bring myself to look at Clay, even when he approached to take one of the coffees, so I handed the cups to Isaac and Kingsley instead.

"I'm going to use the bathroom," I announced, and spun on my heel before any of them could say anything. Had Clay told them all? Perhaps finding out if he was the kind of guy who screwed and spilled was the sort of thing I should have done before I'd slept with him. I don't know why it bothered me so much. After all, it wasn't as though the other guys hadn't witnessed Isaac with his fingers inside me the previous day. I guessed it was just the idea that I hadn't been there—the feeling of being talked about behind my back.

I stalked back up to the café. Heat curled around my throat, spreading across my chest. One of the guys—Lorcan, I thought—called my name, but I ignored him and kept going. I'd get over it, but right now I needed a moment to get myself together. Guys were guys, but that wasn't an excuse. I expected a bit of common decency, even if the rules did seem to be different with me and them.

Keeping my head down so as not to make eye contact with anyone, I went straight to the bathrooms. I'd already spotted where they were while we'd been waiting for the coffee—at the back of the restaurant, through a door, and into a small corridor. The men's was on the left, the women's on the right.

I pushed my way inside the ladies' room, the stench of stale urine and damp hitting me. The café hadn't been great, and the bathrooms were no better. I dreaded to think what the men's was like, but then guys seemed to care less about these things. I wrinkled my nose, but this was better than taking a pee in the bush—just. They were thankfully empty, with no sign of the older women I'd spotted when I'd been lining up with Alex to order. I paused at the sink, placing my hands against the grubby porcelain and letting my neck drop, my head suddenly heavy. I took a shallow breath, not wanting to take a deep one because of my location. Maybe Clay had only told Alex because he thought he could help. I might be blowing it all up in my mind, and it had been a mature conversation between the two of them instead of the ribbing session I was imagining.

I pulled myself together. Considering everything else going on, this wasn't a big deal. I was probably being oversensitive.

I used the toilet, then washed my hands and splashed water on my face. It was one benefit of not having worn mascara for almost a week—I could splash water on my face without worrying about black smearing halfway down my cheeks.

I left the bathroom just as someone was leaving the men's room. I looked up to find a big, round body blocking my way, and my heart dropped. It was the guy from earlier—the older one with the big gut and the filthy smile.

"Well, looky here." He smiled to reveal yellowing, crooked teeth. "Now what's a young lady like you doing out here so early in the morning?"

"I'm with my friends." I tried to step past him, but he moved the same way I did, blocking my way.

"Friends, huh? Is that what they are?"

"Yes, and they're going to wonder where I am if you don't move out of the way."

"I'm not in your way. We're just having a little chat, aren't we?"

The underarms of his t-shirt were stained yellow with old sweat, and I noticed the same color ringing around his neck. "No, we're not. I want to go now."

His eyes narrowed and his lip curled. "Five guys and one girl. What are they doing, passing you around?"

My face burned at how close this disgusting stranger was to speaking the truth. "That's none of your business. Now get out of my fucking way."

"Jeez, you've got a mouth worse than some of the truckers." He laughed. "If you can handle five of them, you can have one extra. Lemme show you what it's like to have a real man."

"Real man?" My lips curled in a sneer, but I was using it to hide how I really felt inside, my heart racing, my stomach coiling in dismay and fear. But I knew you had to stand up to men like him. Show them you're afraid, and they fed on that. Where were the others? I prayed someone else would come in to use the bathroom. "You're disgusting. Get out of my way. Now." I didn't want to put my hands on him to push him out of the way, mainly because I couldn't stand the thought of having to touch him, but that was what I'd do if I had to.

Behind him, the door leading back to the café slammed open and Kingsley's huge shape filled the space. I exhaled a sigh of relief, my shoulders dropping.

The guy gave a nervous glance backward. "Get out of here, we're busy," he bluffed.

But Kingsley moved forward, and close behind him was Clay, his shoulders squared and walking with a swagger. Both of them stepped into the corridor, but someone else followed, and I saw it was Isaac. Isaac kept back for the moment, as though he was overseeing events.

"The lady doesn't look like she wants to be kept busy by you," Clay said.

"Yeah, well, we were just talking. No need to get your panties in a twist."

Kingsley looked to me, his chocolate brown eyes narrowed. "Is that what was happening, Darcy?"

I shook my head. "No, he wouldn't let me leave."

The trucker's head spun back in my direction. "Shut your mouth, bitch!"

Clay barreled forward. "What the fuck did you just call her?"

The man seemed to figure he was in this fully now, and there was no point in backing out. "I think bitch is putting it mildly. I seen her with all you guys. She's a little whore, isn't she?" He looked back to me. "Whatever they're paying, I'll make it double if you come with me."

I didn't even get a chance to tell him to go and screw himself.

Kingsley reached out and grabbed him by the throat, hoisting him up and slamming him against the wall. The man struggled, choking, but Clay moved in, and reached between the man's legs and grabbed the exact spot where his balls would be. The trucker instantly fell still, his eyes widening.

"If you even think about putting your limp dick inside her again," Clay snarled, "I'll make sure I find you, cut it off, and shove it down your fucking throat. Do you understand?"

The man nodded frantically, as best he could with Kingsley's massive fist still around his throat.

Isaac stood back, his arms folded, watching all this happen.

"Can we just go now?" I glanced anxiously at the door. Even though I was relieved the guys were here, I knew the trucker had plenty of friends, and they might come looking for him at any moment.

Isaac's head tilted to one side, his expression cool. "You can go, love. We're just going to make sure our mate here knows exactly what we're talking about."

"I think he got it, guys." My pulse continued to race.

Isaac shot me a look. "Just go."

I wasn't going to argue with Isaac when he had that look on his face. I hurried past them, but paused at the door and glanced over my shoulder. Kingsley dropped the trucker and he fell to the floor, coughing and gasping for air. He was on his knees, curled over, his hands raised as though to say 'surrender.'

Isaac stepped forward, and a flash of metal caught my eye. He had a gun in his hand.

The man spotted the weapon and his eyes bulged, his head shaking. "No, no, please. I've got a wife. A family!"

"Then that makes you worse than scum." He placed the barrel against the man's head. "This is to let you know what we're capable of. If you try to get your trucker mates to follow us down the freeway and cause trouble, I swear to God, you're going to end up with one of these bullets lodged in your pathetic little brain. Got it?"

He nodded. "Got it. I won't say a word to anyone, I swear."

Isaac did that little head tilt I'd come to recognize in him. "Glad we're on the same page." He put the gun away and looked to Kingsley and Clay. "Let's get out of here."

I spun around and hurried from the bathroom, keeping my head down as I passed between tables and my hands in my jeans pockets so no one noticed how much I was shaking.

Only once I'd gotten out of there did I allow myself to breathe, and yet we still weren't out of danger. The truckers' vehicles loomed around us like metal dinosaurs, and I saw how it would be easy for one of them to push us off the road if they decided to exact revenge. That was why Isaac had pulled the gun. Because he'd had to let the trucker know we weren't people to mess with.

Lorcan and Alex both waited by the cars. I assumed they'd remained behind to keep an eye on the vehicles, though it might also have been because Lorcan was still injured and Alex probably thought he'd done something to upset me, which was why the others had been the ones to come after me.

I was shaken from what had happened, but I still gave Alex a smile to show him we were okay. I'd overreacted. Alex had only been trying to look out for me, and, if the six of us remained together for much longer, getting some birth control pills probably wasn't a bad idea.

Lorcan gave me his slow half smile as I approached. "You attracting trouble again, princess?"

"Yeah, seems I can't get away from it."

"The guys handled it, though." It was a statement rather than a question, his gaze flicking over my shoulder as the others followed me down to the car.

I flicked a grateful smile to them, my shaking from the confrontation only just starting to subside.

"Yeah, they handled it."

Chapter Eight

Everyone took a few gulps of their rapidly cooling coffees then threw the paper cups in the trash. None of us wanted to hang around the truck stop any longer than we had to. Hopefully, the man who'd been bothering me would have more sense than to go tell his buddies, but there was always the chance they'd come after us.

As if we didn't have enough to worry about.

We piled back into the vehicles again and peeled out of the parking lot. No one gave chase, so it looked as though Isaac's warning had worked.

My mind went to how hard Isaac had appeared when he'd held the gun to the trucker's head. How many had he killed before? I didn't know how I felt about it. I was glad to have him on my side, but our relationship was still on rocky ground. I never quite knew how he was going to respond to me. One moment, he hated me, the next he was protective. I didn't really know if he was on my side or not.

I took sips from the bottle of water as the car burned through miles, getting closer to home. The guys were professionals and they knew what they were doing, but that didn't stop my nerves. I swung wildly between hoping Hollan was waiting at the house so we could move forward, and praying he wouldn't be anywhere to be seen, so I could feel as though I was getting back to my regular life. But even that thought caused conflict to rise inside me. Did I really want to go back to my old life, where there was no Clay, or Alex, or any of the others? I spent my days plodding through with little direction. I didn't want anyone to be in danger or get hurt, but the idea of saying goodbye to the guys and going back to that nothingness filled me with as much dread as having to face Hollan.

The night sky grew lighter, and, as it did, Isaac turned his attention to the laptop again. He was able to monitor the area around my house, so we'd be better prepared when we arrived, but that didn't mean he wouldn't miss something. He studied the screen for a while, then twisted back and held it up so I was able to see.

"Anything look out of place to you?"

I leaned in closer, scanning the image of the roof of my house, my yard, and the surrounding streets. I watched as one of my neighbors—a middle-management man in his forties who I'd never really spoken to—left his house and climbed into his car in the driveway. The car reversed out onto the road and drove away.

I marveled at the clarity of the image. It must have cost a fortune to gather that kind of data. "Are we seeing this in real time?" I asked.

"As close as we can get to real time. Obviously, there's some lag. The data has to be captured, processed by some seriously powerful computers, and then it's sent to the laptop so we can see it. We're lucky there's no cloud cover today, otherwise we wouldn't be able to do this at all."

"And you have control over the satellite?" My mind boggled at what that meant. It was crazy to think I was looking at the images in real time. The guys weren't just a part of some small vigilante group. This kind of thing took big money.

"It's not solely ours, but we're able to access it if we need to."

"Wow." To get this kind of resolution was crazy, too. I didn't know much about satellite imagery, apart from the few times I'd used Google Earth to look at something, but I knew this kind of resolution wouldn't come cheap.

Were they spies?

Isaac looked up, studying me with that intensity he owned which put me on the side of uncomfortable. "Well?"

"Well, what?"

He sighed, as though frustrated by my lack of understanding. "Is there anything different that stands out to you?"

I refocused my attention back on the screen and shook my head. "No, it looks just like it always does."

"You're sure? No strange cars nearby?"

I shrugged. "I don't exactly have every vehicle in my neighborhood memorized, but as far as I can tell, it's all as it should be." I stared at the screen again, willing Aunt Sarah to come out of the house, perhaps wander down to the mailbox, just so I could check she was okay. A possibility occurred to me. She might not even be there. If Hollan thought she might have information about my location, he might have taken her with him after I'd called.

I told Isaac my concerns, but he shook his head. "She's the best tool they've got to find you. They won't remove her from this location if they think there's any chance of you going to her. And believe me, Hollan won't have given up trying to get his hands on you. Losing you back at the house will only have made him more determined."

My gut twisted at the thought of a more determined Hollan, but then I remembered he was the one who needed to beware of us. We were going to win this and find out what he'd done with the flash drive. It was hard to imagine that he'd had hold of it all these years. It must have been so frustrating to have the drive in his possession, yet be unable to access the information.

"So, nothing looks out of place to you?"

I shook my head. "No, nothing looks any different."

"Okay, let's hope we're getting to the house first, then. Hollan might have suffered bigger losses than we'd anticipated, and it's slowed him down. Stay alert, though. He will be on his way, I'm certain of it."

I nodded, agreeing with him. Hollan had waited years to get his hands on this data. He wasn't going to simply give up.

As we approached the outskirts of the city, traffic began to build, and with it, so did my nerves. I didn't want to admit it, but as well as the possible confrontation with Hollan, I was nervous about seeing Aunt Sarah again. Explaining all of this wasn't going to be easy, especially as Hollan had already been feeding her lies.

Isaac produced a cell phone from his pocket. I thought they'd gotten rid of all the cell phones back at the house, but there must have been replacements at the cabin. He swiped the screen a couple of times then put it on speaker so we could hear what was being said.

Alex answered, and I realized they must have sorted out cell phones for themselves while I'd been in the shower. "What's the next move?"

"I'll go with Darcy and Kingsley into the house. We'll park on the street, but not right outside. Lorcan will stay with the car."

I glanced over at Lorcan to see how he felt about being left behind, but he only nodded.

"What will we be doing?" Alex asked through the phone.

"Circle a couple of blocks. Keep your eyes open for anything that looks suspicious and call as soon as you spot anything, however small it may be."

"Sure."

Isaac hung up and continued to check the satellite imagery on the laptop. I knew he was still looking for any sign of Hollan and his men. The muscles in my shoulders and neck bunched with tension, and I wished Kingsley wasn't driving so I could get him to work out the kinks with those clever hands of his. As I started to recognize my neighborhood, I sat with my fists clenched, my nails digging into my palms. My jaw was rigid, and I ground my teeth had enough to send pain shooting through my jaw. My gaze darted around, watching out for any sign of the vehicles that had chased us from the burning house. Would Hollan be driving the same car, or would he have known we'd be looking out for it and changed it to something unrecognizable?

Everything looked normal. People were leaving their homes to go to work. It was a little early for kids to go to school yet, but I was sure they'd be getting ready inside their homes, packing lunchboxes and eating breakfast. It felt strange to think of the normalcy of other people's homes when my own life had been thrown into turmoil.

We pulled into my street and I sat up straighter, my breath shallow and my heart racing. Nothing looked any different. Was Hollan somewhere nearby, watching? He could easily have access to the same satellite equipment as Isaac, and be watching us arrive right now. I knew the idea of leaving the others outside was to protect us inside the house, and warn us if Hollan appeared to be closing in, but that didn't make me feel any better.

Kingsley pulled over the car and parked up against the sidewalk, beneath a tree. "It'll hide us from the satellite," he said, confirming my fears that Hollan would have the same access as Isaac. The car containing Alex and Clay slid past us, and Clay's stormy gray gaze locked me in for a moment, him twisting in his seat, until they drove out of view.

"We're going in armed?" I asked, unable to keep my nerves from my voice.

"Of course." Isaac picked up his weapon and checked the clip. "Keep your weapon on you, too, but keep it out of view. We don't want anyone to get suspicious."

Kingsley climbed out of the driver's side, discreetly pushing his gun into the back of his pants and covering it with his jacket. He might be trying to look casual, but the size of him automatically drew attention. He looked as though he was a bodyguard to some A-list celebrity.

Isaac mirrored his actions, and I cracked open the back door to join them. I thought Lorcan would have gotten out, too, but instead he climbed between the driver and passenger seat and slid behind the wheel. Lorcan favored his uninjured arm, but his shoulder didn't appear to be giving him too many problems. Of course, he might just be good at hiding the injury. I guessed showing any kind of weakness wasn't a good thing in their line of work. Kingsley had left the keys in the ignition so we could get away quickly if we needed.

We stayed alert, Kingsley at one of my shoulders, Isaac at the other, as we moved at a brisk walk down the street toward my house. In the space in front of me, numbers appeared in my vision. One—the closest, and to the left of my left eye. Four—to the right of my nose, and further back. Eight—behind four, and slightly above. Three—further forward again, and close to my nose.

1483.

The number of my house

I still expected to see something had changed, and though this was the home I'd grown up in, and the house my father had left to me after he'd died, a part of me had detached from the place. It had only been less than a week since I'd left here with Hollan and his men, but it felt like a lifetime ago.

"We'll have to go around the back," I told Isaac and Kingsley. "I don't have my keys anymore, but I've got one hidden." I'd lost my keys at some point during the kidnapping. I had a horrible thought. Had I left them in Hollan's car? Did he now have the ability to let himself into the house whenever he wanted? I made a mental note to tell Aunt Sarah to get the locks changed.

I led the way, and we slipped around the side of the house and into the back yard. On the porch were a number of planters, and inside one of those, hidden by the spray of pink flowers was a small, fake rock with the back door key hidden inside. Sensing the two men watching, I leaned over and picked up the rock, and then flipped open the bottom to remove the key.

I paused at the back door, peering through the glass trying to spot any movement inside. Aunt Sarah was an early riser—unlike me—and would normally be bustling around the kitchen making coffee and breakfast by now, but I couldn't see any sign of her.

Cautiously, aware of the two men at my back, I twisted the key in the lock and pushed open the back door.

I went to move through, but Kingsley pressed me back and moved past me to enter first. I knew what that small movement meant. He thought there was a chance Hollan was already here and, if he was, Aunt Sarah was already in danger, or worse—hurt or even dead. A hollowness appeared inside my chest and ballooned outward. I couldn't stand to think of anything bad happening to her. She was the only family I had.

While Kingsley protected me from the front, Isaac had my back. We moved as one unit into the kitchen. An empty mug sat on the table, and I reached out and touched its porcelain sides. It was cold. She hadn't drunk from the cup that morning. I check the coffee pot as well, just to be sure, but it was clean and unused.

Had Hollan taken Aunt Sarah from the house? Was she not even here?

A creak of a floorboard came from overhead, and we all froze, our eyes lifting to the ceiling. My stomach squirmed with anxiety. Was it her, or was it the sound of Hollan's men waiting for us, one of them making the mistake of shifting his weight and so alerting us to their presence?

Kingsley started toward the door which led out into the hallway and the staircase. He put out an arm to tell me to stay back, but I wasn't going to hide in the kitchen. Both he and Isaac had pulled their guns, and I did the same, planning on defending myself, and the two men, if I had to.

Following Kingsley's broad back, I stepped out into the hallway. The front door was farther down the corridor, the staircase to our left. Kingsley led us to the bottom of the stairs. Movement came from the top of the stairs, and Kingsley pointed his weapon. "Don't move!"

There was a small scream and, recognizing the voice, I released the air from my lungs. "Aunt Sarah!"

She stood at the top, clutching her robe around her body, her eyes widened at the big man pointing a gun in her direction. Her gaze flicked to me and she blinked a couple of times, as though she wasn't quite sure if she was dreaming.

"Darcy?"

I went to run up the stairs to greet her, but Isaac's hand around my bicep stopped me. "We don't know it's safe yet."

"Are you alone, Aunt Sarah?" I asked urgently. "Is Hollan or any of his men here?"

The confusion on her face deepened, and she shook her head. "No, they left straight after you called the other night." I saw the timeline of events of the past few days sweeping across my vision, and the moment where I'd picked up the phone and called Aunt Sarah pulsed out toward me. "What is all this, Darcy?"

"I'll try to explain." I pushed past Kingsley to meet her on the stairs, slipping the gun I was holding into the waistband of my jeans so I had both hands free. "It's so good to see you."

We pulled each other into a tight hug, then I leaned back to look into her face. "When I didn't see you up already, I thought the worst might have happened."

My comment seemed to perplex her. "I'm off sick because you're supposed to be missing, Darcy. And with everything that's been going on, I haven't been sleeping well, so I guess I'm not exactly sticking to my schedule." Now that she'd said it, I could see the darker shadows bruised beneath her eyes, the extra lines deepened around her mouth, as though my disappearance had added years to her skin.

"Of course. I'm so sorry." I said it as though this was my fault, as though I'd had any choice in any of the events that had led me up to this moment.

"What happened to you? Who are these men?" Her gaze flicked over my shoulder to take in Isaac and Kingsley behind me.

"I can explain, but we don't have much time," I told her. "Are you able to get dressed and pack a small bag with your things? We need to get out of here."

"What are you talking about?"

"Hollan isn't one of the good guys, Aunt Sarah. Please, just trust me about that. He was the one who killed Dad. I saw him that night, but I'd been in a state of shock and it hadn't registered with me."

She gave a bark of laughter. "Don't be ridiculous. Special Agent Hollan was your father's friend."

"No, he pretended to be Dad's friend. Please, you have to trust me. He might be here any minute, and then this is going to get dangerous."

"It already is dangerous." Kingsley's deep voice came from below us. "We need to get moving."

Something in my expression must have made her realize I was serious, or maybe it was just harder to say no to Kingsley.

"Okay, give me ten minutes to get ready," she said. "I'll meet you in the kitchen." More lines appeared between her brows. "But I expect an explanation for all of this, Darcy. I've gone through absolute hell over the last few days."

I didn't like to leave her alone, but she wouldn't want me hovering over her while she got dressed. She reversed the way she'd come, pulling her robe tighter around her angular form, as though it could protect her against what was to come. I felt wretched about putting her through all of this, but I had to keep reminding myself that it wasn't my fault. I hadn't asked for any of this either.

I remembered how I'd been looking forward to getting some of my own clothes again. I felt as though I'd been living in other people's clothing for months now, even though it had only been a week, and my jeans were so filthy they could probably get up and walk off on their own.

"I'm going to get changed as well." I twisted to look over my shoulder at the two men waiting at the bottom of the stairs. "I need my own clothes."

Isaac nodded. "Okay, but don't take long."

"I won't."

They both watched me with equal intent, and I had to tear my eyes away to focus back on the stairs.

I reached the top, then crossed the landing, passing by my aunt's bedroom door, hearing her moving around behind it, before reaching my own. I pushed open the door.

Seeing my bedroom again caused a wave of nostalgia to hit me, stealing my breath. How was it possibly so little time had passed since I'd last been in this room? I felt as though I was a different person now, and the girl who'd left here a week ago was a far younger, far less wise person than the one who'd returned. I'd never been a girly-girl, and I'd long ago gotten rid of many of the items I'd owned as a child—soft toys and fluffy pink cushions—and had replaced them with funkier items, mainly technological. There was also a framed photograph of me and Aunt Sarah taking a rare selfie, but other than that, there weren't any photographs. Most women my age would probably have pictures of their friends, but I hadn't gotten close enough to anyone to want to have their photograph in my bedroom. My makeup, most of it a year old and worn down to the plastic container, was scattered across my dressing-table. I had a couple of Yankee candles, the sweet vanilla scent permeating the air, and a framed print of an artist I'd loved when I'd been in my teens was hung on the wall. A full-length mirror was positioned in the corner of the room, a couple of shoe boxes of heeled pumps which I never wore, balanced beside it.

Snapping myself out of my reverie, I got to work. I took the gun out of the waistband of my jeans and placed it on the dressing table, between the half empty lipsticks and eye shadow pots. Peeling off the dirty jeans and t-shirt I wore, I headed to my chest of drawers. I paused with the t-shirt in my hand. It was Alex's, and I wasn't sure if I was supposed to give it back. I'd launder it when all of this was over, I decided. I could return it then.

I owned about ten pairs of almost identical jeans, so picked out a new pair. I also took a pair of panties and a bra out of my underwear drawer, and hurriedly swapped the borrowed underwear for a clean set of my own. I finished the outfit with a simple, fitted black t-shirt. I was torn between wanting to look good and being practical. I didn't think any of the guys would appreciate a woman who cared more about her looks than making a quick getaway, if needed.

I hesitated for a moment, then grabbed a backpack off the hook on the back of my bedroom door where I had a variety of belts, scarves, and purses hanging. I took it back to my drawers and pulled out a second set of clothing and underwear, then threw in a hairbrush and socks for good measure. A final stop at my bathroom allowed me to add my toothbrush and deodorant to the bag as well.

Finally, I picked my gun back up and placed it in the waistband of the fresh set of jeans, then tugged the black t-shirt down over the top to hide the grip.

With the backpack slung over my shoulder, I took the stairs back down to join the men, who were still waiting for me. I figured I'd give Aunt Sarah a little more time to get ready.

"Better?" Kingsley asked me, his eyebrows raised. I caught his gaze, sliding up and down my body, but coming to rest on my face.

"Yeah, much. Thanks."

Isaac remained silent.

We went back into the kitchen, and Kingsley sat in one of the chairs around the table, dwarfing the item of furniture, the wood vanishing beneath his big body. Something caught my eye, and I shifted the backpack on my shoulder, then reached to the center of the table and picked up the folded wedge of notes. In front of my vision, the number two, followed by two zeros, flashed up. It was the money I'd been paid by the journalist. If I knew how to keep my mouth shut, none of this would ever have happened. I still hadn't figured out if it was a good or a bad thing.

Isaac took out his cell phone and called Alex. "How's things out there?"

"Quiet, as far as we can tell. And inside?"

"The aunt is here. We'll be back out with you in five."

"Make it quick. This is all a feeling a little too easy."

"Yeah, I hear you."

I didn't like the way they were talking, and my stomach turned over uneasily. Were they thinking this might be an ambush? "Maybe Hollan just has something else to be doing?" I said, hopefully.

Kingsley heaved out a sigh and sat back in the chair. "I'd like to make you feel better, Darcy, but considering the current situation, I'd say that's unlikely."

"Where is he, then?" I challenged.

Isaac's teeth dug into his lower lip and he shook his head. "I wish I could tell you."

I bit back a growl of frustration. All this access to information, and yet they couldn't keep track of one man.

Chapter Nine

The kitchen door opened, and both men automatically reached for their weapons. But Sarah stepped through, dressed now in a long-sleeved t-shirt and slim-fitted jeans and boots. Her short hair had been spiked with some kind of gel, and she frowned at the men from behind her glasses. "Am I going to have a gun pointed my way every time I walk into a room?" She looked down her nose disapprovingly.

"Sorry." Isaac lowered the gun, but didn't make any move to put away his weapon. "We can't let our guard down."

Like me, she'd packed a bag. She set her small hold-all down beside the kitchen table, and Kingsley went to pick it up for her.

"Leave it," she said. "I'm quite capable of carrying my own bag. Now, is someone going to explain to me what the hell is going on?"

Isaac shook his head. "Not here. We need to get both you and Darcy somewhere safe before Hollan shows up."

Her lips thinned, her nostrils flaring. "That man has been in my house almost every day since Darcy went missing, and he's never so much as spoken sharply to me. Yet you boys show up here, waving guns and making demands, and it's you I'm supposed to listen to?"

I'd had a feeling Aunt Sarah wasn't just going to go along with things.

"Please, Aunt Sarah," I tried. "We're all telling the truth. Hollan is dangerous. He murdered your brother, and now he's after me because I have information he wants. That's why he's been here. After I called the other night, he traced my location and sent armed men after me. We were lucky to make it out alive."

She shook her head, her blue eyes wide behind her glasses. "This all sounds crazy, Darcy. You know that, don't you?"

"You need to trust me on this. If we don't leave, you'll be in danger."

Lines appeared between her eyebrows. "From Hollan?"

"Yes!" I was starting to lose my patience. I was also starting to understand why the guys had just snatched me the way they had. I'd have most likely given them the same sort of response Aunt Sarah was giving me now, and she had *me* here to clarify things. They'd have been trying to explain the situation without any allies on their side.

Isaac's phone buzzed and he answered, putting it on speaker so the rest of us could hear. "What's going on?"

"Not sure," came Alex's voice, "but a chopper has just gone overhead. Might be nothing, but I think we probably need to get out of here."

Isaac hung up without saying another word.

Kingsley got to his feet to head to the back door.

"We're leaving," I told Aunt Sarah. "You have to come, too."

Isaac glanced over and then lifted his weapon a fraction. "We will make you, if you don't do as you're asked, but please understand that you're forcing our hands."

I winced internally. I didn't want him to take the hard-handed route with her. But then I reminded myself that Hollan could hurt Aunt Sarah to get to me, if he wanted, and we needed to do whatever was necessary to keep her safe.

Her eyes hardened, and she glanced between me and the gun. She was probably hoping I'd tell Isaac to put the weapon away, but I couldn't do that. Force was never going to be a first choice, but if it had to be a final and only option, then so be it.

"I'm sorry, Aunt Sarah, but we really do have to go, and you're coming with us."

Her shoulders dropped, and she huffed out a breath of frustration. "Very well."

Thank God.

She picked up her bag from the table, the one she wouldn't let Kingsley carry. She was a stubborn one, that was for sure. But I would be relieved to get out of here. I wasn't sure what would happen now—if we'd head back to the cabin, or if we'd remain watching for if or when Hollan showed up—but I felt better knowing she was safe.

From outside, the muffled thrum of helicopter blades sent vibrations through the air.

My heart skipped in my chest. The chopper Alex had spotted. "Is it Hollan?"

Isaac looked to me, his lips a thin line. "Not sure, but I don't want to hang around and find out."

Surely Hollan wouldn't start shooting at us from a helicopter in the middle of the city? Even the police wouldn't resort to that in a built up, residential area.

But urgency pressed on my back, and, with Kingsley leading the way, we left the same way we'd arrived. In our small group, we hurried out to the front of the property. Lorcan had moved the car so it was right outside the front of the house, and we all ran for it just as Clay and Alex pulled up behind.

Isaac opened the driver's door. "Move over," he told Lorcan.

Lorcan did as he was told and scooted across to the passenger seat, allowing Isaac to climb behind the wheel. I assumed Isaac figured if we needed to make a quick getaway, having someone with an injury driving wasn't the best idea.

The rest of us crammed in the back, me and Aunt Sarah first, with Kingsley squeezing in beside me. We wedged our bags down by our feet. It occurred to me that we'd have been better spreading out to the other car, but I guessed Isaac wanted more men in the car in case something happened. He wouldn't want to leave Aunt Sarah and me unprotected.

Isaac pulled away from the curb quicker than normal, but not enough to draw attention, and Alex and Clay followed.

The steady hum of the helicopter grew louder, and I twisted in the seat to try to spot it in the sky. There it was—a dark shape against the blue. "Shit, is it following us?"

"We might need a plan." Kingsley leaned forward to address Isaac. "If it's him, he might be waiting until we get to a less populated area before he makes his move."

Isaac nodded as he drove, focusing on the road ahead. "Then we need to be on the offensive instead of the defensive. Let him come to us, and we'll be ready for him."

Lorcan spoke up from the passenger seat. "What about Darcy and her aunt?"

"Hey, I'm armed," I protested. I didn't like being spoken about as though I wasn't there, and as though I was defenseless. "I can fight."

"You're what he's after." Lorcan's voice was curt. "We need to protect you, both of you, not put you in the middle of things."

Kingsley looked to me. "Seems to me like we're already in the middle of things."

I craned my neck to catch sight of the helicopter again. They must have gotten clearance for the chopper. In the current climate, you couldn't just fly aircraft into the airspace above the capital. That the government might be on Hollan's side made my stomach twist. We could very easily be painted as the bad guys, while Hollan came out of this smelling of roses.

The traffic slowed, trapping us between vehicles on every side. The inability to move, combined with the claustrophobia of having people and cars closing us in, caused my anxiety to skyrocket. My knee bopped up and down, and I clenched my fists, open and shut.

I peered out of the window again. The helicopter had moved farther away, but was still visible—a black semi-circle with blades and a tail. From this distance, I was unable to tell if the aircraft belonged to any kind of establishment, the colors painted on its side indistinguishable. Could we be completely wrong and it was a news helicopter, or even a traffic chopper. We were in rush hour now. We might be wrong about this whole thing.

My aunt must have picked up on my anxiousness. "What's going on, Darcy?"

"Hollan is most likely after us." I reached out to squeeze her hand. "They're just trying to get us somewhere safe."

She spoke low, as though that would help Isaac and the others not hear her, even though we were sitting only inches apart. "And who are *they*?" She lifted her fine eyebrows, and I noted how, despite the urgency to leave, she'd still taken time to draw them on.

"It's kind of hard to explain right now." I wished I had an easy answer for that question. "They keep an eye on authority figures who look like they're crossing a line."

"Shouldn't the police be doing that?" She frowned. "Or the FBI?"

"Sometimes it's the police or the feds who are the ones who need keeping an eye on."

Her eyes widened behind her glasses. She was a smart woman. She knew what I was telling her—that these men worked below the radar.

The traffic continued to crawl forward, but the helicopter remained buzzing back and forth above us, like a wasp at a picnic that refused to go away.

"This is Kingsley." I gestured to where he was sitting beside me, and he twisted to nod at my aunt.

"Ma'am."

"The guy in the passenger seat is Lorcan."

Lorcan lifted his hand in greeting. "Hey."

"And the one driving is Isaac." I hesitated and then added, "And he's the one in charge."

Isaac didn't say anything. He was driving and must not want to be distracted. I guessed he had to concentrate. He pulled around one vehicle and got in behind the next. I glanced back to see Clay and Alex following, and a car blasted its horn as their vehicle cut in front. The helicopter stayed with us.

Isaac pressed his lips together. "We need to get out of sight of that chopper."

Worry fluttered inside me. "You really think it's him?"

"Yeah, I think so."

"Me, too," Kingsley agreed.

I bit my lower lip. "Shit."

"I'll take George Washington downtown. See if we can lose them there."

I frowned. "Shouldn't we be trying to leave the city, not head further downtown?"

Lorcan spoke up. He only seemed to speak when there was something of importance to say. "That's what Hollan will want us to do. Get us out in the open and away from people. He won't want witnesses, and we won't be able to run with him following us like this."

We took the bridge across the river, the second car containing Clay and Alex following us. Isaac's phone buzzed, and Isaac handed it to Lorcan to answer. Lorcan did so and then put it on speaker.

Isaac leaned over to speak. "Alex?"

Alex's voice came through the phone. "What's the plan, Isaac?"

"We have to get rid of this chopper. You seen any other vehicles following?"

"No, I don't think so."

"They're probably using the satellite as well. We need to dump the cars."

His voice was tinny through the speaker. "Where? The moment we do, they'll see us."

"Stay close. I've got an idea, but be prepared to react quickly. It may not work."

"What are you going to do, Isaac?"

He didn't reply.

"I don't like this," Aunt Sarah said. "I think you should let me out."

Kingsley twisted toward her once more. "If we do that, Hollan will pick you up, and then we can in no way guarantee your safety."

"I don't think you can do that anyway," she replied.

No one answered her. She had a point, but I knew there was no way Isaac was going to let her out. He'd lock the car doors and put a gun to her head if he had to. He had it in him to do so.

We reached the other side of the river, following the line of cars into the city. Still the chopper hovered above us, always maintaining enough distance to keep sight of us, without getting so close that we'd be able to get a good look at them. They must be FBI. There was no way they'd be allowed this close to the White House's airspace without clearance.

Isaac took Pennsylvania Avenue, the vehicles four abreast. He swerved in and out of traffic, pushing the car as fast as he could without causing extra attention from the cops. We didn't want to get pulled over for traffic violations right now.

Ahead of us, the rectangular mouth of the 3rd Street Tunnel yawned, the road starting to curve downward.

"Everyone buckled in?" Isaac called back.

My heart tripped. "What are you planning?"

"Just brace yourselves the moment I say so."

What the hell? I reached out and took hold of Aunt Sarah's hand. She gave me a worried look, and I squeezed her fingers, trying to give her reassurance I didn't feel myself.

We entered the tunnel with its tiled walls and dim lighting. I checked behind again, making sure Alex and Clay were still with us. They were close behind. Despite knowing Isaac was planning something, a tiny part of me relaxed, knowing we were hidden from the chopper during the time we spent in the tunnel. We'd emerge soon enough, however, and then what would we do?

The end of the tunnel got closer, opening out into bright white daylight. I could also now see the oncoming traffic on the opposite side of the road as it entered the tunnel traveling in the opposite direction. Where the two flows of traffic had been divided up until this point, there was a gap in the barriers as we began to leave the tunnel. Only a strip of tape and a few cones, perhaps left over from a previous accident, separated us from the other side.

"Brace!" Isaac suddenly yelled.

Instinctively, I grabbed hold of Sarah, using my arm stretched across her body to pin her back against the seat. Before I could even scream, Isaac wrenched the steering wheel and swung the car through the gap. Brightly colored cones flew into the air, one of them bouncing off the windshield, and tape fluttered like a kite that had lost its gust of wind. Isaac yanked the car hard so it spun into the direction of the oncoming traffic to go back into the tunnel on the other side. Horns blared.

An SUV clipped the back of the car, throwing us forward, and sending us spinning into traffic. I screamed, tensing against what I was sure would be another car hitting us. All around us, a cacophony of brakes screeched, and horns blared as the traffic was brought to a standstill. It felt as though the car would never stop moving, but it did, sideways, blocking the traffic behind us.

Clay must have had quick reactions, as I glanced back to see their car had managed to follow us.

"Everyone out," Isaac yelled, throwing open the car door and climbing out. Neither Kingsley or Lorcan hesitated for a moment, their doors swinging open so they exited the car as well. The vehicle we'd hit had also ended sideways, blocking more of the traffic. A man in his thirties, wearing a suit, climbed from the car. He looked unhurt but confused about what had happened. Other vehicles tried to crawl by on the outside lane, more concerned about not being late for work than if anyone had been injured during the 'accident.'

"Come on, Aunt Sarah," I said, scooting along the seat to the open door, grabbing her hand to drag her with me. "We've got to get out."

She was pale, and I saw her long, slim hands trembling. "What on earth is going on, Darcy?"

"We have to do what Isaac says."

I gave her hand another tug. "Please, Aunt Sarah. They know what they're doing." I sure as hell hoped that was true. "And we can't just sit here."

Traffic was quickly building behind us. My point got across to the rational part of her, and she jerked her head in a nod and started to follow me out. I climbed out and then helped her from the car, so we all stood in the road. I glanced back to see Clay and Alex running toward us, weaving between stationary cars.

The suited guy shook his head at Isaac. "What the hell happened?"

Isaac reached into the back of his pants, where his gun was hidden, and pulled the weapon. "Sorry mate, but we're going to need your car."

The suited man's eyes widened. "What?"

"You heard me." Isaac gestured with the barrel of the gun. "Now move."

The man put his hands into the air. His vehicle was a seven-seater, and would easily fit all of us. The front was dented where it had hit Isaac's car, but would still run.

"Quick, everyone in," Isaac yelled to us. "Before Hollan realizes anything's wrong."

He would soon enough, when the traffic build-up from this end of the tunnel became more noticeable. Though he'd seen us enter from the other side, he'd figure out soon enough that we hadn't emerged. I pushed Aunt Sarah forward, toward the other man's car. I couldn't see the confusion on her face, but I couldn't have her asking questions and fighting me. We just needed to do what Isaac said.

"Come." Alex appeared at Sarah's side and took her elbow. With her other hand, she clutched the bag she'd brought with her from the house. With a sinking in my stomach, I realized I'd left my backpack in the car, but there wasn't time for me to go back and grab it. "We need to move quickly."

She glanced up at him. There weren't many women who wouldn't be dazzled by Alex's blond haired, blue-eyed good looks, and she allowed herself to be led toward the car.

"Hey, that's my car!" the suited man cried, more confused about what was happening than angry.

"You'll get it back," Isaac said, gesturing with the gun again. "We're just borrowing it."

He jumped behind the wheel. I slid in beside Sarah, and the other guys climbed in, too, Clay and Alex in the third row, Lorcan beside me, and Kingsley in the front. Though it felt as though we'd been swapping cars for ages, probably less than a minute had passed.

Doors slammed shut around me, and Isaac brought the engine back to life. He shoved the SUV into gear and stamped his foot down on the accelerator. It had only been the traffic behind the vehicles that had been brought to a standstill, so the route ahead, which was also heading back the way we had come, was free from traffic apart from the few cars that had managed to slip through.

What Isaac had planned suddenly dawned on me. If Hollan was in the chopper, then he would have seen us driving into the tunnel in two separate black cars, heading west. We were about to leave the tunnel heading in the opposite direction, with all of us in only one car, and it was a red SUV they wouldn't think to look for, never mind recognize. Yes, Hollan must realize there was something going on, especially when the traffic slowed and we didn't appear from the end of the tunnel, but this would give us enough time to get away.

Chapter Ten

We burst out of the other end of the tunnel, back into daylight.

I had no doubt the guy we'd just carjacked would be on the phone right now, calling the cops, which would include the description and license plate of his vehicle, so we didn't have long. We needed to dump the SUV and find something new, but only once we'd put some distance between us and the chopper.

I craned my neck, trying to spot the helicopter. I caught sight of it between the towering, gray buildings of the city skyline, but it was farther away now, and on the east side of the tunnel, waiting for us to appear. I pictured Hollan's face as it dawned on him that we'd given him the slip, the anger and disbelief contorting his smug features.

Isaac kept his foot down, putting more distance between us and the chopper. The moment the opportunity arose, he left the freeway and drove down the smaller side streets, leaving downtown and the helicopter containing Hollan behind us. Even though we were driving a stolen car, I found myself relaxing a little. I glanced over at my aunt to try to smile at her, but she stared resolutely ahead, deliberately not making eye contact with me. The weight of worry pressed on my chest, making it hard for me to breathe. Yes, we'd managed to lose Hollan for the moment, but Sarah had just witnessed us causing a car accident and then stealing a vehicle.

Isaac's voice broke my train of thought. "We're going to need to dump this vehicle, or the police are going to be on our tail." He spoke loud enough for us all to hear. "I'm sure Hollan will be able to tune into police radio. He'll put two and two together, and figure out what we did soon enough."

"We'll be better on foot," Clay called from the back, leaning forward in his seat.

Isaac nodded. "Yeah, I think you're right."

Despite knowing we needed to lose the car, Isaac pushed on, increasing the miles between us and the helicopter. I could barely see it from the rear view now, the buildings surrounding us obscuring the skyline, so I only caught the occasional glimpse, and I no longer heard the thrum of the blades.

Within ten minutes, Isaac pulled into a residential area and parked the SUV. It was a smart area, with mature trees planted at uniform distances along the sidewalk. The townhouses were attached to each other, but individual steps led up to elegant front doors, and I couldn't see anyone loitering around. These kinds of places were owned by professional people, and most would already be at work by now.

Isaac twisted in his seat to address us. "We should probably split up. We'll be less noticeable that way."

His words sent a jolt of adrenaline through me. "No, we're not splitting up." I hated the thought of not knowing everyone was safe. "We need to stick together."

His lips twisted, his brow drawing down in a frown. He considered my words then exhaled through his nose. "Okay, but we need transport. Move quickly, but don't run. We don't want to look suspicious."

The group of us—five gorgeous guys, plus me and my aunt, who was in her fifties, made me think that we already looked like a strange group, and we were bound to draw some attention, but I didn't say so.

Each of us climbed out. We left the stolen car behind and hurried down the street, putting several blocks between us. Not only did we not want to get caught with the car, each of us, except Aunt Sarah, was also armed, and I didn't think that would go down too well with the cops if we gave them any reason to want to search us. I felt vulnerable on foot, however. Isaac periodically yanked at the doors of the parked cars we passed, trying to find one already unlocked, I assumed, to steal.

"Hey, can't we just use Uber and get a cab?" I suggested, starting to get out of breath. I knew Sarah would be struggling to keep up, too. She was physically fit from her cleaning job, but the strides of the men were far longer than ours and we both had to jog to match their pace, Sarah clutching her bag against her chest.

Isaac glanced over his shoulder at me, and I thought he was about to tell me not to be an idiot, but a rare smile tweaked the corner of his lips, and he slowed. "Dammit. Why didn't I think of that? We'll get a cab out of the city, at least, and I'll get base to arrange new vehicles for us. Then we can figure out where to take Darcy and her aunt where it will be safe."

A rush of pleasure at his praise rose inside me, but I quickly quashed it. I didn't need Isaac's approval.

"Or we could just take them both back to base," Kingsley suggested.

Alex frowned. "They're civilians. We don't let civilians know that location."

"These aren't normal circumstances," Kingsley continued. "And we know they'd both be safe there while we track Hollan down."

I looked between them as they spoke. I wanted to point out that we didn't need to track Hollan down—he was in a helicopter hovering above the city—but it wasn't as though we could get to him while he was up there. I also understood the pressing need to keep my aunt safe. While I was happy to put myself in danger to get to Hollan, I wanted her to be somewhere well out of his reach.

"I don't think the boss is going to like it." Isaac frowned.

Kingsley shrugged. "Maybe not, but sometimes you've got to break the rules a little to do the right thing."

I thought there had been plenty of rule breaking going on. Didn't seem to me like Isaac had any problem on that front.

"Let's get the cabs first, and then decide," Isaac relented. "We're not all going to fit in one, so we're going to have to separate." He shot a look in my direction, and I knew the next line was meant for me. "But it will only be for a short while. We'll meet up at the outlet mall on the other side of the river. There'll be enough people around, it'll allow us to vanish into the crowd. We won't get noticed and it won't get flagged up by the cab drivers as somewhere strange to take us."

I wasn't sure about that. Five beefy guys heading to an outlet mall probably wasn't something they saw every day. But then I realized we were splitting up, and so we wouldn't be so obvious.

At any sound or movement coming from above, I found myself lifting my face skyward, checking for the helicopter again. We needed to get off the streets. Our descriptions would be circulating by now. I didn't want to risk us being spotted.

Isaac used his phone to call for the cabs. The compact layout of the city meant that one was with us within minutes.

"You go first," Alex encouraged us. "We'll be right behind you."

I knew they'd be less noticeable without us, but that didn't mean I felt any better about leaving Alex and Clay standing on the side of the street.

"Just go, sugar," Clay said softly, nodding in the direction of the waiting cab as though he could read my thoughts.

I had to think of Aunt Sarah. She'd been worryingly quiet throughout this whole thing, which wasn't like her at all.

I gave Clay a final smile then followed the others into the waiting cab. A part of my heart was left behind on the street as the door slammed shut and the cab pulled away from the sidewalk. I lifted my hand in a backward wave to Clay and Alex, my neck twisting as I watched them grow smaller through the rear window.

They look too vulnerable just standing there, though I knew they were perfectly tough, capable men. Plus, they were both armed. That wouldn't mean much if someone started shooting at them from a helicopter, however.

Anxious, I leaned forward. "How long is the second cab going to be?"

"It's coming soon," the driver said. "Few minutes, that's all."

"Chill, Darcy," said Kingsley. "They'll be fine."

I sighed and sat back.

The flow of traffic heading out of the city was better than it had been as we'd been going in, and we made good progress. Within twenty minutes, the cab pulled up outside the mall. I noticed Aunt Sarah remained quiet, and I wondered what was going through her head. She wasn't normally someone who held back on what she thought, and I sensed a storm brewing.

We climbed out, Isaac paying the driver. People milled around, many clutching takeout cups of coffee, others already holding bags with store names scrawled across the front. People ate breakfast and sipped coffee while perched at the outside seating of a couple of restaurants. Wooden planters and young trees interspersed the brick and concrete. A small fountain was supposed to give the calming sound of running water, though the melodic tinkle was drowned out by the music from the various stores, the chatter of early shoppers, and vehicles parking nearby. It would be easy to blend in here, though, and allow us to regroup and decide what was going to happen next.

Were they really going to take us to whoever was Isaac's boss? I didn't know how I felt about that—nervous and unsure. I wanted the five guys back to myself again, and didn't want to have to deal with anyone new. What if their boss said I wasn't allowed to join them when it came to taking down Hollan? He could block me out of this whole thing.

The taxi drove away, and we waited for Alex and Clay.

"Can you call them?" I asked Isaac, clenching and unclenching my fists, my neck craning for any sign of their cab.

He nodded and pulled out his phone. He swiped the screen a couple of times and then placed it to his ear. Someone must have answered right away as he said, "Hey, how are you doing?" He waited for a moment, listening to the reply, and nodded. "Okay, nice one. See you in ten." Isaac looked to me. "They're on their way. Let's get coffee and breakfast while we wait."

"Yeah," Kingsley agreed. "I could eat a horse."

He looked like he was capable of eating one, too.

My aunt raised her hand as though she were in school. "I'd like to find the bathroom, if that's okay."

"Sure," Isaac said. He jerked his chin toward Kingsley. "You can take her."

She folded her arms, her lips pinched. "I'm a fifty-four-year-old woman. I'm more than capable of taking myself to the bathroom."

"Yeah, sorry." Isaac shook his head. "Not happening."

"I'll go with her," I volunteered. "I could do with going myself."

Isaac looked between us. "I still want Kingsley to go. It's a precaution. He won't come in with you, just make sure no one suspicious is around."

I looked to Lorcan, hoping for a bit of backup, but he shrugged his apology. I understood their concerns. My aunt didn't exactly buy in to all of this yet, and we didn't know how far Hollan had spread his net. I thought we were pretty safe, having lost him downtown, but there was always the risk we'd been followed. Plus, I remembered the incident with the trucker the last time I'd been to the bathroom. Maybe Isaac was more worried about a repeat of that happening than he was about what Aunt Sarah might do, or Hollan's people showing up.

"It's okay," I told her, catching her eye and holding it. "It's better this way."

She pursed her lips and glanced away in a way that told me it wasn't okay. What else could I do, though? Let her go home and allow Hollan to get her?

I touched her arm. "Come on."

Knowing there wasn't much more we could do, she allowed me to guide her into the mall. I looked for signs for the bathroom, spotted them, and followed the directions. Kingsley stayed a couple of steps behind us, and I couldn't shake the feeling we had a bodyguard.

We reached the door which led onto the bathrooms, and I turned to Kingsley. "We won't be long."

He nodded. "I'll be right here."

I led the way, pushing inside. A woman was standing at the sinks, fixing her lipstick. She glanced over and gave us both a small smile, before smacking her lips together then moving past us to leave.

Sarah spotted the window on the other side of the bathroom and left me to hurry over to them. She reached up to where it was ajar a couple of inches, and started to yank at the top.

"What are you doing?" I hissed, glancing anxiously back at the door.

"Seeing if there's any way out of here."

"You can't do that!"

She gave another look at the window, which hadn't budged. "Apparently not," she replied, though it wasn't quite what I meant.

"It's okay," I said, helpless, unsure what she was even trying to escape from. "It's only Kingsley out there."

My aunt put her hands on her non-existent hips. "I really don't like this, Darcy. I know you want me to trust you, but please try to see it from my point of view. You go missing for days, have the FBI asking after you, and then you turn up with men who think nothing of waving guns around and stealing cars. You tell me Hollan was responsible for killing your father, but where is the proof?"

I tapped the side of my head. "It's in here, Aunt Sarah. I remembered seeing him. I caught his reflection in the glass door while Dad was dying, but I must have been so traumatized, I blocked it out. But Kingsley helped me to remember it all. He's a trained psychotherapist.

He hypnotized me, and I remembered, just like I remembered the code dad gave me before he died. That's the reason Hollan is after me now. He's got the memory stick dad took, but it's encrypted with the code he told me."

Her lips were pinched, the fine lines around her mouth spanning out and deepening. "How much can you trust this Kingsley? You say he hypnotized you into remembering, but have you ever heard of fake memories? A clever therapist can put ideas into your head, so you think you remembered something, but it was actually planted by him."

I remembered thinking something similar when hypnosis had been suggested to me, but I still shook my head. "No, they wouldn't do that. I trust them."

She spoke in a harsh whisper, trying not to be heard while also trying to get her point across. "Why? Isn't it convenient for them that you trust them and give them the code, and think Hollan is the enemy? What if he isn't, and these men are the bad guys? What if Hollan is keeping the memory stick safe from them, and he wants to get hold of you to keep you safe, too."

For the first time, a thread of doubt sewed across my heart. No, that wasn't how it was. And yet I couldn't stop my mind from going to how this whole thing had started. They'd held up Hollan's vehicle, had shot FBI agents, then taken me and kept me in a cellar for three days. If I was looking in on this situation, I'd be telling myself to run for the hills as well.

Could I really trust them at all?

The idea filled me with a deep unease that I didn't want to think about too hard. My aunt had a point, and she didn't even know about the 'being held in a cellar' part. I imagined she'd beat the crap out of the guys if she ever found out. And while I completely understood her point of view, I couldn't believe they were the bad guys. I'd seen how they'd looked at me, how they'd touched me, and spoke to me. They acted as though they cared, but was that just a part of my fucked up brain? Had they twisted me during my time in the cellar? I'd worried about Stockholm syndrome, where a captive ends up sympathizing with their captors in order to get through their ordeal, but I didn't think I was actually a victim.

I didn't want to lose my trust in them. Didn't want to lose *them* at all.

My anger toward my aunt grew. "You don't know what you're talking about. It wasn't a fake memory. I was there, and you weren't. I saw Hollan in the house the same night Dad died!"

"Maybe he was taking the memory stick to keep it safe?" she suggested. "If you did see him, you don't know he was there for a bad reason."

I glared at her, my fury ice cold, lodging in my heart. "He left me there, holding dad in my arms as he died. He didn't stop to help us—to help *him*. It was the neighbors reporting gunshots and glass breaking that called the police there, and they were the ones who found me. He was dead by then. You know that, don't you? If Hollan was there, he let a man die in his teenage daughter's arms. You think those are the actions of a good man?"

She shook her head, took off her glasses, and rubbed her hand across her face. "After you went missing, Special Agent Hollan waited until he was invited into the house, and then he gave me nothing but help and reassurance."

"Aunt Sarah, Hollan is the one I've been hiding from."

"Honestly, Darcy, I don't know what to think right now. This whole thing is all kinds of messed up."

"Yeah, I'm perfectly aware of that."

My tone was cold. A part of me wished I'd never bothered coming back to the house. I'd only done it because I'd wanted to protect her, though the guys had done it because they'd thought my aunt could be used to get to me. I knew what I was most angry about, and it wasn't only that she didn't fully believe I'd seen Hollan that night. I was angry because she was trying to change the way I felt about the guys, and I didn't want that. Not even in regard to Isaac.

I cared about them, and the thought surprised me. I got the feeling they cared about me, too, but maybe that was the Stockholm syndrome coming into play? Was it possible to still have Stockholm syndrome days after you'd been allowed to walk free? I could understand if I was someone who'd been kept for years, but not after a matter of days.

We fell silent as another woman pushed into the bathrooms. She gave us a cursory glance, and we pretended to wash our hands until she vanished into one of the stalls.

"Even if I agreed with you—which I don't," I added hastily, "Isaac and the others aren't just going to let you go home."

"And that doesn't tell you everything you need to know?" she said, giving me that same look as she used to when she knew I'd done something wrong as a teenager. "Men don't get to tell a woman what to do, just because they're bigger and have a gun."

I hardened my jaw and lifted the back of my shirt. "I have a gun, too, Aunt Sarah."

Her eyes widened. "What are you doing with that, Darcy?"

"They gave me one to protect myself with. This isn't about them trying to use us. They are genuinely trying to protect us."

She sighed. "I don't know what to think anymore."

A bang on the bathroom door made us both jump. "Everything okay in there, ladies?" called out Kingsley's familiar baritone voice.

"We're coming," I chirped. I shot my aunt a look that I hoped told her to behave herself.

We'd had a role change, with her the one most likely to cause trouble, for once.

Chapter Eleven

We left the bathroom, and Kingsley shot me a quizzical look. I shook my head briefly, widening my eyes to try to tell him not to say anything. Thankfully, he kept his mouth shut and didn't question why we'd taken so long.

Together, the three of us went back to where Isaac and Lorcan were waiting. I was relieved to find Alex and Clay had already arrived.

Alex gave me a smile and a nod, and Clay slung his arm around my shoulder and yanked me against his side.

"There you are," he said. "We missed you."

I grinned up at him. "I missed you guys, too."

I felt better having the two of them here again. A part of me felt unnerved when we were all apart, like important parts to an otherwise well-oiled machine were missing. Was that how the others had felt when Isaac hadn't been with them when I'd first been taken? Was that why they'd been so unsure of how to treat me?

My aunt's words wiggled like maggots through my head, trying to infect my brain. These weren't the bad guys, no matter what she thought. I was sure of it.

Isaac looked to Kingsley. "Everything all right?"

Kingsley nodded. "Sure."

Why did I feel like a lot more was said in that small exchange of words? I watched as Isaac's gaze flicked to my aunt, who still stood with her arms folded and her lips pinched. They were worried she was going to cause trouble, and, truthfully, so was I. At least she hadn't tried to get the attention of the mall security or anything yet. If she did anything to get the others in trouble, I'd feel responsible.

"So," Kingsley said, "what's the plan?"

"He's sending someone in to pick us up. They shouldn't be too long."

"That's good." His gaze flicked to Aunt Sarah. "And what are we doing with Darcy and her aunt?"

"They're coming with us."

His eyebrows lifted in surprise. "To the base?"

"I assume so. I didn't get much more information other than to hang out here and that they are sending someone to extricate us."

"Okay. We might as well get comfortable while we wait. Any idea on the ETA?"

"Should only be an hour. Not much more."

"Well, I'm starving," I said, putting my hand to my stomach. "Did we even have breakfast? I'm losing track of meal times." I looked to Sarah. "You must be hungry, too. We whisked you out of the house before you'd had time to eat."

I wanted to take care of her, but wished I could shake the guilt. I felt it from all sides—from the guys for getting my aunt involved in all of this, and from Aunt Sarah for putting her through everything. Deep down, I knew it wasn't my fault, but that didn't stop me feeling that way. A part of me also wished I'd never had to pick up my aunt in the first place. Things had felt less complicated—or at least as uncomplicated as they could be in this situation—when I hadn't needed to take her opinions into account.

Clay jumped up. "I'll grab a heap of coffees and breakfast sandwiches as takeout from the coffee shop over there. I'm gonna guess we don't want to eat in just in case our ride shows up."

"That sounds like a plan," Alex said. "I'll give you a hand." He looked to me. "You want to come, Darcy?"

I did, but leaving Sarah alone worried me. I shrugged. "Nah, I'd better stay here."

My aunt knew me too well. "I'm sure I'll be fine for ten minutes, Darcy. I don't need to be supervised." Trouble was, that was exactly what I thought she needed, and I hadn't had the chance to tell Isaac that she didn't trust any of them yet. I suspected he was smart enough to see it in her, but my concerns about her yelling for help, or trying to get the attention of a mall cop or security were valid.

I offered her my most winning smile. "I'd rather stay here with you."

Her eyes narrowed just a fraction behind her glasses, perhaps not enough for the others to notice, but she and I knew each other too well, and we both knew exactly what the other one was thinking.

CLAY AND ALEX RETURNED with seven hot sandwiches wrapped in greasy paper. The smell made my stomach rumble. Bacon, egg, cheese, and sausage. There wasn't a single vegetable in sight, and as I took my first massive bite, the grease dripped from my lips, and, self-consciously, I wiped it from my chin, knowing it would make my skin shiny. The coffee was strong and sweet, and though I'd only had a few hours' sleep, I was starting to feel more alert.

Where was Hollan now? I imagined how pissed he'd have been when he found our two vehicles abandoned in the tunnel. He'd figure out what had happened quickly enough, but would that mean he'd give up searching for us for the day? He'd have access to traffic cameras and perhaps would have been able to track the car we stole to the point where we'd gotten the cabs, and then to here. Though it might take him some time to access all the information. By the time he'd gotten hold of it, I hoped we'd be long gone. I was aware that while Hollan wanted to find us, we also needed to find him. He still had the memory stick, and without that, the code was completely useless. But he'd had the huge advantage of a helicopter today, and I knew it wasn't the right time. It's not as though we'd been able to start shooting at the aircraft. We needed to try again, though I didn't know how or when.

The guys all wolfed down their food, licking fingers and giving groans of satisfaction. "I could have eaten ten of them," Kingsley said.

Sarah handed him her still wrapped sandwich. "Here, have mine."

I frowned. "You have to eat, Aunt Sarah."

"Really, I'm not hungry."

I widened my eyes at Kingsley to try to tell him not to take the sandwich, but he ignored me and plucked the food out of her fingers. Within less than a minute, the second sandwich had vanished. I guessed with Kingsley's size, he must need twice as many calories as a regular person.

The mall had gotten busier as we'd sat outside eating, people shopping and chatting with friends. We looked like a group of people just hanging out, but I noticed how alert each of the men were, even while they'd been demolishing their breakfast, and I knew their firearms were close to hand should anything look suspicious.

A large black van pulled up outside the front of the mall.

I stiffened, sitting up straighter, my pulse racing. I glanced over to the men to gage their reaction, though they'd all noticed the van's arrival, none of them appeared worried.

Isaac got to his feet. "I think our ride is here."

I allowed myself to relax a fraction. If Isaac thought it was safe, then it most likely was.

A man, who appeared to be in his late thirties, jumped out of the driver's side. He gave a nod to Alex then opened the side of the van. The large door slid out and then across, revealing rows of seats inside, clearly intended for moving larger numbers of people.

My aunt picked up her bag, and I was amazed she'd managed to keep hold of it through all the drama. "This isn't making me feel any better about things, Darcy," she hissed at me as the guys all headed toward the vehicle.

"You're safe, I promise," I tried to reassure her, though my promises felt empty. There was no way I could actually guarantee her safety.

"I'm going along with this because I love you," she replied. "No other reason."

I gave a half smile, one that covered the sadness that rose inexplicably in my chest. "I know. Thank you. I hope you'll be able to look back and see that everything we did was for the right reasons."

"I hope so, too, Darcy."

I reached out and gave her hand a squeeze.

We piled into the van, with Alex going first and then putting out a hand to help Sarah up, which she took begrudgingly. I followed her in, and then came Kingsley, followed by Clay and Lorcan, who appeared to be holding his injured shoulder again, and then Isaac.

The driver slid the door shut and climbed back behind the wheel. He hadn't said much to us so far, and I wondered if Isaac and the others knew him at all.

There were no windows along the side of the van, only the windshield allowing any light in. It meant we weren't able to see out, but also meant no one else knew the vehicle contained people rather than building supplies or some other transit material. I was relieved to be leaving the city behind, especially now that we had my aunt safely with us, though I knew this wouldn't be the end of our ordeal. Hollan wasn't going to just give up, and neither would Isaac and the guys.

For that matter, neither would I.

I sat with Kingsley's big shoulder wedged up against mine, but, instead of squashed, having him next to me made me feel comforted, protected. That, combined with the low light in the back of the van, and the distinct lack of sleep I'd been getting recently, caused my mind to drift.

Chapter Twelve

My eyes flickered open, and I realized I'd been sound asleep with my head on Kingsley's shoulder. I quickly wiped at the side of my mouth, hoping I hadn't drooled all over him while I'd been sleeping. My hand came away dry, and I allowed the flutter of panic to die away inside me. That could have been embarrassing.

"Hey." He glanced down at me with fondness in his deep brown eyes. "You're awake, so I can move now." He rolled his shoulders, the muscles in his neck rippling as he did so.

"Sorry. You should have woken me."

He gave a chuckle. "I'm only teasing. You looked adorable ... mouth open, snoring."

I jabbed him in the ribs. "I do not snore!"

He winked. "Course you don't."

I resisted the urge to deliver another elbow to his side. Blinking the sleep from my eyes, I looked around at the others. Lorcan was also sleeping, his head resting against the side of the van. I hoped his shoulder was okay. Maybe Alex should check it again when we stopped. The guys might all be tough, but running around like that when you'd only recently been shot couldn't be good for a person. Isaac was staring at his phone, that usual small frown causing lines between his eyebrows as he concentrated. Alex sat with my aunt beside him. Sarah stared resolutely ahead, and though I tried to catch her eye, she wouldn't look at me. She blamed me for all this, and was probably worried about what was coming next. I was only able to see the back of Clay's head, and didn't know if he was awake or sleeping.

"How long have we been driving?" I asked Kingsley.

He shrugged. "Couple of hours, I think."

"A couple of hours?" I parroted back. "I didn't think I'd been asleep that long."

"You obviously needed it."

"Yeah, I did. How much farther have we got to go?"

"Not too long now."

I wondered where exactly we were going and who would be waiting for us when we got there. Were we being taken to another safe house, like the place that had burned down, or the cabin? They'd mentioned a 'base,' but I didn't know what that meant. Were we driving to another city, where there would be a high-tech building they worked from? The limited view out of the vehicle was frustrating, and I sat up straighter, trying to see over the tops of Clay's and Lorcan's heads, and past the driver, to catch sight of any road signs that might give me a clue about our location. Other than being a couple of hours outside of D.C., I didn't have any idea. I guessed I could ask now. It wasn't as though I was being kept prisoner.

"Where is this place?" I asked Kingsley, keeping my voice low. I told myself it was because I didn't want to disturb those sleeping, but it was really because I didn't want Isaac to pay attention to me.

He looked at me side on. "I don't think I should be telling you that."

I rolled my eyes and sighed. "Seriously? I wish you'd start trusting me."

"I do trust you, Darcy," he said, twisting to face me as fully as he could in the confined space. "But it's something that affects too many people for me to be the one to make that decision."

I looked around at everyone else in the van. "What if they all agreed?"

He shook his head. "It's bigger than us, even. I'm sorry."

Not wanting to push him, I fell silent. Surely once we got out of the van, I'd have some idea of where we were. I could check out street signs, or see if the address was written on anything. It wasn't as though I'd be completely in the dark. A thought occurred to me—unless they planned on putting a bag over my head, of course. My stomach dropped, but not because I was worried about myself. Aunt Sarah wouldn't think much of it if they tried to cover her face as well. She already thought they were a bunch of thugs, and putting a bag over her head would only cement that idea.

Though my view of our surrounding area was limited, there was enough to be able to see that we'd left the city far behind. An expanse of trees stretched on either side of us, and I wondered if we were going back to the cabin. But I was sure we'd left the city in a different direction—from the west—and I hadn't spotted anything I recognized from the drive down here. We were higher up as well, the flatter ground morphing to hills and valleys, which were only increasing in both size and altitude.

We stopped for a comfort break, but there was nothing around. No bathrooms or coffee shops. Only more trees, and us on the side of the road. No other vehicles passed us. I stepped into the forest, just off the road, to relieve myself behind a tree, thankful for the dappled shade. Aunt Sarah insisted she was fine, but her silence worried me. She'd never been someone to hold back on what she thought before.

I figured we were in a national forest, though I wasn't sure where. Past Harrisonburg, perhaps? Sleeping for so long hadn't helped my sense of direction either, but the remoteness and height of the surrounding hills and mountains made me wonder. What were we doing all the way out here? This was the sort of country where you could hike for days and only come across a handful of people. I struggled to see what Isaac and the guys would be doing all the way out here.

We drove for another hour, heading deeper into the wilderness.

The driver, whose name I didn't even know, and who'd barely spoken the entire trip, leaned back in his seat to address us. "We're here, folks."

I looked over at the guys expectantly, part of me thinking they were going to crack up and start punching each other on the shoulder at the great joke they'd just pulled on me, but it was a different kind of smile on their faces—wistful, thoughtful, content—as though they'd just come home after an extended trip away.

Isaac turned, but he was addressing Sarah and me rather than the other guys. "We're going to have to walk the rest."

The driver climbed out, and the side of the van was pulled across to let us climb out. My feet hit the ground, and I straightened up, my hands on my hips as I surveyed the area. We were in a small clearing in the forest. Around us, trees had been felled, leaving only stumps. The tree trunks lay stacked horizontally in piles, but as far as I could see, there wasn't much else here. A couple of other vehicles, all built to carry a number of people, were parked a little farther on. None of them was new, all with mud splashes, scrapes down the paintwork, and dents in the hood and bumper.

"It's this way." Isaac jerked his head toward the track which led higher up the mountain.

I looked back to the driver, who was busying himself by shutting the side of the van again. "Is he coming?"

"Nah, he's got other places to be."

We started to walk, Isaac leading the way. His smart clothes, which he must have found and changed into at the cabin, appeared in contrast to the surrounding area, as though someone had picked him straight out of the city and dumped him in the middle of nowhere. Kingsley and Alex also appeared a little too smartly dressed to be hiking, and Lorcan, while in a more suitable jeans and t-shirt combo, seemed to be struggling.

Of all the guys, Clay appeared the most comfortable in his surroundings. Like a dog let off the leash, he bounded ahead, a fresh bounce to his usual swagger. He cupped his hands to his mouth and let out a whoop of pleasure that sent birds bursting from the trees. I didn't know what we were doing here, but just seeing him like that made a ball of happiness swell inside my chest.

We rounded a corner of the cleared path.

A gate blocked the way. It seemed strange to have a gate in the middle of nowhere, especially when the fence it was attached to only ran a few feet in each direction.

A sign was attached to the wooden struts.

PRIVATE PROPERTY
DANGER
LOGGING IN PROGRESS
TRESPASSERS WILL BE PROSECUTED

My aunt spoke in a low voice. "What are we doing here, Darcy?"

I twisted my lips and shrugged. "I'm not entirely sure."

The others all seemed to know where they were going, however, and they took off up the hill, ignoring the no trespassing sign and slipping through the gate. I was glad Aunt Sarah was physically fit from her job, and, as we took after the men, she kept up pace with them. That didn't stop me wondering the same thing, however. What were we doing here? Admittedly, it was a good place to hide out from Hollan until we decided our next move, but when Isaac mentioned about going back to their base, I was picturing something a little more like Langley.

Reddish-brown chunks of rusted metal appeared alongside the track, pock-marked with holes and falling to pieces. I had no idea what they'd been in a previous life, but they weren't much good for anything now. As we grew closer, the sense of dilapidation and abandonment grew, and, with it, my sense of confusion. The guys appeared confident, knowing where they were going and not giving me any impression that they were seeing anything they didn't expect.

We rounded a corner and were faced with huge pieces of machinery that had long been abandoned. Metal struts covered in a rash of the same orangey-red rust towered above us. An old pulley was corroded into place. They were hulks of machines that looked as though they'd given up and died right where they were.

I was becoming more confused by the moment.

"What are we doing here?"

Clay hooked his arm around my shoulders and grinned. "You'll see."

I arched my eyebrows. "That's not an answer."

One person had been falling behind, and I turned my attention to him. "How are you doing, Lorcan?"

I noticed he'd been holding his shoulder again, his face taut with concentration as we'd walked. I wondered if he'd pulled open his wound, or perhaps had an infection. He wore his leather jacket, so it was impossible to see if he was bleeding, but he definitely looked as though he was going backward, health-wise.

"I'll be better when we get inside," he replied, his voice as tense as his expression.

Inside? Inside where?

I looked around, half expecting a building to materialize, but none did.

Isaac approached the rusted machinery. I wanted to call to him to be careful. That stuff didn't look stable, and I exchanged a worried glance with Sarah. Our concerns came from two different places, however. I was worried about Isaac, where she was more troubled about us.

He leaned over, pushed a few fallen branches, twigs, and leaves out of the way, and then did something I couldn't quite see, though it looked as though he was entering a pin code into a cash machine. Then he spoke, apparently into the ground. "Hey, it's us. Let us in."

Something clicked, and a mechanical whirring thrummed through the ground. I glanced over at the guys. No one seemed surprised.

A hatch, similar to the one at the cabin, only this one made of metal rather than wood, lifted out of the ground, and out of the hole it left, a metal box began to ascend from the earth.

My mouth dropped open. "What the hell?"

The box drew to a standstill, and the mechanical thrumming faded away. I suddenly felt as though I'd stepped into a sci-fi movie. The metal box was taller than Kingsley and looked as though it would fit perhaps four people comfortably inside, six at a squeeze. It looked like an elevator, but was of course missing the usual shaft and pulleys. I wondered where it had come from, but assumed it led down to the base they'd been talking about.

"I'll take Darcy and her aunt first," Isaac said. "The rest of you follow after."

I guessed I was about to find out.

"What about Lorcan?" I said. "He's not feeling great. He should go down first." Of course, I had no idea what I was sending him down to, but there had to be more help down there than there was up here.

Lorcan shook his head, but I noticed the beads of sweat across his forehead and upper lip. It might have just been from the exertion of the walk, but I thought it was more than that. "I'm fine. I can wait a few minutes."

Alex turned his attention to the other man. He placed his hand on Lorcan's forehead, though Lorcan frowned and jerked his head away. Alex got enough of a feel to make a judgment, however. "Your temperature feels a little high. Are you getting more pain?"

Lorcan snorted. "More pain than a bullet being lodged in my arm?"

Alex remained serious. "You know what I'm asking."

Lorcan's defenses dropped. "Yeah, it's hurting more than it was."

"We'll get you checked out as soon as we get down. You might need antibiotics."

This time Lorcan didn't give him an argument, and it made me wonder exactly how bad he was feeling. I didn't know what lay beyond the metal doors, but I hoped it would involve help for Lorcan.

The doors of the metal box slid open, confirming my suspicions of it being a type of elevator. A panel of buttons was on the right-hand side, and I wondered where each of the keys would take us.

Isaac stepped forward, leading the way, before glancing back over his shoulder and jerking his chin to tell me to move.

My heart pattered in my chest and my mouth ran dry at the thought of what was about to happen. It looked like we were about to be dropped straight into the bowels of the earth, though the elevator appeared high tech and well maintained, even though this was the last place I'd ever think there would be one.

Without feeling I had much choice, I took Aunt Sarah's hand, her fingers tightening around mine, and together we stepped inside.

Chapter Thirteen

Somewhere deep below us, a mechanism began to whirr.

Isaac stepped in to join us and hit a button on the keypad. The doors slid shut, blocking my view of the surrounding forest, the old logging equipment, and, most importantly, of Lorcan, Alex, Clay, and Kingsley. My heart tightened at having to leave them behind, not liking being solely in Isaac's presence, but I reminded myself this would only be a short time, and we'd all be reunited soon.

The elevator jolted, causing my grip on my aunt's hand to tighten, and then we were moving down, into the bowels of the earth. Or at least that was how it felt. I glanced over at Isaac, but he stood staring straight ahead, not giving anything away, though I was sure I caught the faint hint of what appeared to be a smug smile tugging his lips. He was enjoying this—keeping me on my toes, surprising me—I could tell.

My pulse quickened in anticipation as the doors slid open to reveal a room of high tech equipment beyond. This was like the cellar at the cabin, only on overdrive. A couple of rows of computers were in the center of the room, people I didn't know working at them. They looked up as we stepped in, and then went back to their work. More screens showing various moving images covered the walls, and among them I spotted the footage of the group remaining outside. We were obviously being watched while we'd been out there. I wondered about the locations the rest of the screens were showing—a city, a house, an ocean vista. What was important about those places that they needed to be monitored by a group of men quite literally working underground?

A tall, dark-haired man, who'd been looking up at the bank of screens as we'd entered, turned to face us. He stepped forward to greet us, a welcoming smile on his handsome face. His gaze flicked over me, but he put his hand out to Isaac first.

"Isaac, it's been a long time."

Isaac smiled—one of the first full and genuine smiles I'd ever seen from him—and took the offered hand. "Yeah. It feels strange to be back."

The man was older, somewhere in his forties, I guessed. Definitely a generation above the other guys. His eyes were a deep blue, and his dark hair was flecked with white at the temples. He was dressed smart-casual, in pants and a light blue shirt. His stubble was more designer than lack of shaving, lines creased from the corners of his eyes, and there were more across his forehead. I didn't need any more gorgeous men in my life right now, and I figured this particular one was too old for me anyway, but that didn't stop me from admiring his qualities. Plus, Isaac clearly thought a lot of him, and Isaac was a hard man to impress.

Behind us, the elevator rose again, to bring the others down, I guessed. I tried not to think too hard about the layers of rock and earth above our heads. This place looked like it was built solidly, but it still felt unnatural being underground.

"Devlin," Isaac continued, "this is Darcy, the girl all the excitement has been focused around."

The man nodded slowly to me, almost a bow. "Darcy. You're Michael Sullivan's daughter." It wasn't a question. He reached out his hand to me, and I placed my fingers in his. Instead of shaking, he squeezed my hand. "We owe you an apology for failing your father. He should never have been put in the position he was in. I know it's all too little too late, but I hope we're going some way to trying to rectify that now."

I wasn't sure what to say. I didn't think locking me up in a cellar for three days was any normal person's way of making an apology, but these weren't exactly normal circumstances.

"Thank you."

He gave my hand a final squeeze. "He was a good man."

I couldn't stop the smile springing to my lips. For so long, I'd questioned that exact thing, and even though I'd known the truth in my heart, it didn't stop my head turning the way everyone else said he'd betrayed our country over and over. I glanced across at Sarah to see if his kind words had affected her in the way they had me, but she still had that pinched expression, and I felt a prickle of irritation. Swallowing my emotions, I gestured to my aunt to introduce her.

"This is my dad's sister, Sarah."

He directed his charming smile in my aunt's direction. "Of course." He put out his hand to shake hers and she took it, though I sensed her reluctance. "I apologize for the interruption to both of your lives. I understand this must be difficult to get your head around."

Sarah glanced at her surroundings. "What is all of this, anyway?"

He continued to expose her to his flawless smile, not dropping the expression for a moment. "Why don't we show you both around?"

The elevator opened behind us, and the other four stepped out, Alex with his arm around Lorcan. Lorcan's face was pale, and sweat had beaded across his brow, as though just taking the elevator had been a massive effort for him. I frowned at the sight, not liking seeing Lorcan going downhill, but I was glad they were all here with us now.

Alex didn't stand on any ceremony. "I'm going to get him down to the medical bay."

My frown deepened, and I looked to Lorcan, who only appeared embarrassed by the whole thing. "Is he okay?"

Alex's lips pressed together in concern, his nostrils flaring. "I think it's an infection."

Lorcan lifted a hand and shook his head. "I'm fine."

He didn't look fine, and worry threaded its way through my heart.

"He just needs some meds," Alex continued "He'll be feeling himself again soon enough."

"I am right here, you know," Lorcan said, but I heard the weak amusement in his voice. Lorcan was a man of few words, but he could obviously tell when someone was caring for him.

"We were just about to give Darcy and her aunt the tour."

Kingsley stepped in. "I can help show Darcy and Sarah around."

"I'm here, too." Clay lifted his hand into the air, as though he were at school.

Isaac nodded. "Okay. I've got some things I need to discuss with Devlin. If you could both show them around, that will give me some time. Give them a room each down on Middle 2, near to our rooms, okay?"

"Sure thing, boss." Clay threw me a wink. "I'll make sure Darcy has the room right beside mine."

I narrowed my eyes at him and tried to hide my smile.

Devlin raised a hand to garner our attention. "Sorry to do this, boys, but before you go anywhere, you need to unarm yourselves." He looked to me. "You, too, Darcy, if you're carrying. The only weapons we have down here are the ones used during gun practice. You can have the guns back again when you leave."

I understood what he was saying—that we weren't allowed to take our weapons down with us into the rest of the base. I guessed it was their way of keeping people safe.

Reaching into the back of my jeans, I pulled out the handgun I'd been given. The guys around me all unarmed themselves as well, sliding the weapons onto the desk beside Devlin. Devlin raised a hand again, and gestured to one of the other men working here, who came forward with a large plastic box and began to pile all the guns inside.

"They'll be safely under lock and key until you're ready to leave again," Devlin said.

I wasn't sure how I felt about the guns being taken away. I had felt safer in the outside world while I'd been armed, but we weren't going to come to any harm down here. My reason for wanting to carry had been fear, but there shouldn't be anything or anyone to be afraid of now. The fact the guys had handed over their weapons without any protest also made me feel better.

Alex had disappeared with Lorcan back inside the elevator. Isaac was already speaking to Devlin, their voices low and heads pressed close together. I guessed this was the same person he'd been speaking to when we'd been back at the cabin.

"Come on, then," said Sarah, stiffly. "Let's see what else is in this place."

We waited for the elevator to come back up then stepped inside. I glanced at the pad containing the buttons for the other floors, I assumed. Instead of only numbers, they were labeled B, M2, M1, and U.

"Bottom floor is for teaching and training," explained Kingsley, pressing the next one down. "Middle 2 is the sleeping quarters, and the one I'm taking you to now is Middle 1, which is our living area. We've just left Upper." The elevator light pinged and the doors slid open. Kingsley stepped out, continuing to talk, and we all followed him. "This is where we live. We have a TV room, a gym, a dining room and kitchen. It's not too different to how we'd live in a regular house."

Being deep underground seemed nothing like living in a normal house, but I didn't want to point that out to them. "Have you spent a lot of time here, then?"

Clay chuckled beside me. "You could say that, yeah."

He showed us from room to room, a TV room that looked more like a cinema. A large dining hall with numerous tables, a kitchen that looked like a professional kitchen you'd find in any restaurant. Even the gym looked impressive, not that I spent much time on treadmills or lifting weights. I thought Kingsley must have spent a lot of time in here in the past.

"You can help yourself to anything you want while you're here," Clay told us. "Treat the place like your own."

"And how long are we going to be here?" asked Sarah.

Clay shrugged. "Dunno. Until we figure out the next move, I guess. Isaac and Devlin will come up with a plan, and I'm sure they'll let us know when they do. Until then, we're safe down here, so we might as well make the most of it."

The guys took us down to the floor below, and we walked down a corridor of doors. "You can have the rooms at the end," Kingsley said. "There are enough for one each. They're basic but clean. When people have been here for any length of time, they make them their own, but neither of you will be here long enough for you to need to do that. We'll get all of this sorted before then."

He made it sound as though we were here because of a gas leak or flood, rather than someone chasing us with helicopters and guns.

Curious as to what the rooms looked like, I opened the door and stuck my head inside. The room was sparse. A bed, that wasn't quite a double but was bigger than a single, with starched white sheets. A chest of drawers. A bedside table holding a lamp. Two other doors led off the room, and I crossed the floor to check behind them. One door led to a shallow wardrobe, and the other to a tiny bathroom containing a shower, toilet and sink. Of course, being underground, there weren't any windows.

Aunt Sarah stood in the doorway, also curious to see what the rooms were like. Kingsley and Clay lurked behind her, peering over her head as though to garner my reaction.

"Where are your rooms?" I asked the men.

Kingsley pointed to the door directly across the hall. "I'm in that one."

I smiled. "Right across from me."

He nodded. "And, Sarah, you can have the one next to Darcy."

Sarah breathed in deeply through her nose. "Right. And what am I supposed to do about my job while I'm hiding down here? I have people who are dependent on me."

His eyes narrowed in confusion, lines appearing between his eyebrows. "I thought you cleaned for a living."

I flinched and tried to give Kingsley a glare, but he was focused on my aunt.

"I do," she snapped. "People rely on having clean homes and businesses, you know."

"Sure. Sorry, I didn't mean anything by it."

I didn't blame her for being mad. She worked her ass off, and to have someone make out like the job she did wasn't important was insulting. I guessed from Kingsley's point of view, with his degrees and qualifications, it seemed like a crappy job, but when you've worked hard to build up a reliable business, it didn't matter what that business was—you still put your heart and soul into it.

"You okay?" I asked her quietly as I left the room, Kingsley and Clay walking ahead, leaving us to follow along.

"I guess I have to be."

"Your business will hold over a couple of days. I'm sure you can make some phone calls if you need to let people know you're away."

She shook her head. "I don't like this, Darcy. We're essentially being kept prisoners down here."

"No, we're not. They're protecting us."

She *tisked* at me. "You can't trust everyone you meet simply because they say what you want to hear."

My mouth dropped. "I don't!"

"Just be careful, Darcy. I see how those boys look at you. It makes me wonder what they want from you, and I can't pretend I'm comfortable with all of this."

"They take care of me, Aunt Sarah. They care about me, too, I'm sure of it. You know how it feels when you're with someone you care about, just like I know I care about you."

Her expression was hurt, her tone irate. "I care about you, too!"

"I know you do, Aunt Sarah," I said, softening. I'd put her through hell, not just now, but over all the years she'd been looking after me since Dad was murdered.

She continued. "And sometimes caring about someone means making hard decisions—decisions you know the other person isn't going to be happy about, but ones you know are right."

I nodded eagerly, glad she was finally seeing things my way. "That's exactly why we had to come and get you. It wouldn't be safe any other way."

She sighed, but nodded in agreement. I hoped this was the start of her defrosting a little. She'd always been a tough woman, but I didn't like feeling as though there was a divide between us, especially not now.

"We'll show you the bottom floor," Clay called over his shoulder, "but you can't stay for long, okay? Everyone will be busy, and they're too easily distracted."

What had they said was down there? Training, wasn't it? I guessed it would be more computers …

We caught the elevator down. The doors opened, and we stepped out into another corridor. Several doors led off the corridor, with long windows stretching between them. The glass was only partially obscured by vertical blinds, the slats half open. Clay jerked his chin at me to tell me to join him, and then he nodded toward the first window. I moved to stand at his side and peeped through the glass. An adult stood at the front of the room, going through what looked like arithmetic on a whiteboard. Sitting at desks in front of him were five boys, all around a similar age—seven or eight years old.

Clay started to walk again and gestured at me to follow him. We passed the second door and stopped to look through the window of the next room. This room contained older boys—early teens—and they stood around waist high benches containing glass beakers and Bunsen burners. Protective glasses covered the boys' eyes while the flames from the burners danced high in red, orange, and yellow. The strangely familiar and emotive scent of methane and burning chemicals assaulted my nostrils, instantly transporting me back to my own high school years.

We might be however many hundreds of feet beneath ground, but I recognized a science room when I saw it. These were classrooms.

Clay jerked his head toward the rest of the corridor. "Come on. There's more to see."

I smiled at his enthusiasm. It reminded me of when he'd shown me around the house, how he'd seemed to take pleasure in doing so, exposing me to new things. The memory couldn't be untied from the way he'd kissed me at the top of the stairs either, though I highly doubted he'd do that again now, especially not with my aunt present.

We followed Clay up the corridor and came to stop on the opposite side from the other classrooms. These windows looked into a far larger space. Inside were boys I guessed to be around twelve years old. They were in a sports hall, though it was far smaller than you'd find at a regular high school. There wouldn't be any basketball games played here. Not that they looked like they were playing that kind of sport. No, the boys, though dressed in regular shorts and t-shirts, were clearly practicing some form of martial arts. They were standing in pairs opposite each other, throwing punches, kicks, and blocking with their arms up, or ducking in defensive moves.

"We're taught how to handle ourselves in a hand to hand combat situation, as well as everything else," Kingsley said. "With what we do, it's almost as important as learning mentally."

I nodded. "Of course."

We continued to walk, leaving the fighting boys behind.

The door directly ahead was different from the others, in that it had no glass panel, and a light beside it. Right now, the light glowed green, but I assumed it showed red on occasion.

"That's our shooting range," Clay said. "It's where we learn gun safety, maintenance, and of course, how to shoot."

I'd spent time on a gun range in my past, both as a child and after my dad had been killed. Guns would never be my most favorite of things, but they were necessary, and at least I knew how to handle one.

"We don't need to go in there," I said, "I know what a gun range looks like." Besides, it seemed pointless going in there if it was unoccupied.

I still had questions, however. "If the boys are all trained here to do what you do, what happens if they don't want to take this path in life? Do they get to say if they want out? What if during all this training, they don't perform like they're supposed to? Do any of them not make it?"

Did any of them decide they wanted out, or were they all so institutionalized that they didn't know there was the possibility of them living any other life?

Clay regarded me, his eyebrows raised. "And that's a lot of questions in one breath."

Kingsley stepped in. "No, they don't all make it. Not that many drop out voluntarily, of course." He regarded me, his deep brown eyes suddenly sad. "You don't know how it feels to be an older boy caught in the system. You get passed from place to place, and with each move you get angrier and more expectant of being moved on, so you just act out to make it happen already. As a kid, you're told to not take candy from strangers, but we were asked to live with them and call them Mom and Dad."

My heart broke at his story, and I reached out and squeezed his fingers. But I was starting to see why the boys would choose to live down here when given the choice.

"But you said some don't make it?"

Clay shrugged, joining the conversation. "Things happen. Kids get sick. There are accidents."

"What happens to those boys?"

"They live here until they're eighteen, unless they want to leave early, in which case they go back into the system. Once they leave, they're free to do whatever they want. They're set up with some money and somewhere to live, and they're sworn to secrecy, of course, but otherwise their lives are their own."

It was good to know the guys had had choices. Yes, they'd been steered in this direction, but if they'd really decided it wasn't for them, they'd have been able to do something different.

They had called it training, but ultimately, I was looking at an educational space. That, combined with the bedrooms, and the dining room, and kitchen, plus the recreational areas, made it clear to me that everything had been provided for the boys to not only live, but thrive down here.

There was only one thing missing.

Family.

I turned to Clay and Kingsley. "This is where you all grew up? Where you were brought after the foster homes?"

They glanced at each other with a rueful smile, and both shrugged. "Yeah, this was home," Clay said.

I'd almost forgotten about my aunt, but Sarah was staring in at the boys. Her expression was tight, her nostrils flared and her lips pressed together. "The children live down here?"

I looked to her. "Yes, Aunt Sarah. But the boys down here don't have family of their own. They were taken from foster homes, where they were unwanted, and brought here to have a different kind of life."

Her frown deepened. "But it's not normal to have boys living like this."

Clay stepped in. "Honestly, living in foster care isn't exactly normal either. At least here we felt like we were something special—chosen—instead of being the ones nobody wanted."

That seemed to placate my aunt.

Kingsley glanced in at the boys. "Each kid here is given a good education, then taken off individually to be shaped into whatever thing they've shown a talent or special skill or interest in."

I wrinkled my nose. "How are any of the kids supposed to know what they are most interested in, or what they want to do? I'm twenty, and I still don't know what I want to do."

"You forget that we were already showing an interest or a skill in something before we were brought here," Kingsley pointed out.

Clay shoved his hands deep into the pockets of his jeans. "Yeah, I was taking things apart for as long as I can remember. If it came to pieces, that's what I'd do, and then I'd put it back together again. It would keep me entertained for hours. I don't know how I knew how to do it—I'd never been taught at that point. I just had an instinct for it."

I liked to think of Clay as a small boy, sitting cross-legged on the floor, his blond hair falling into his face, with tons of little pieces of metal around him. Had his real parents looked at him fondly when he'd done that, or had it driven them bat shit crazy to buy him something new, only for him to take it to pieces? What had the response of the care home been? I imagined they'd have been less lenient with him. I wondered what had happened to his folks for him to have ended up here. There was so much I didn't know about their pasts. Strangely, the one I knew the most about was Isaac.

What about the others? Had Kingsley shown signs of being more caring? Had Alex been interested in how the human body worked? I didn't like to think of Lorcan showing a particular interest in guns, but maybe that was what happened? And Isaac, with his computers? I imagined Isaac as a child—bossy and wanting for things to always go his own way. Had the boys clashed when they'd been brought here, or had they been friends?

Kingsley frowned at me. "What are you thinking?"

I snapped myself out of my thoughts. "Just about what you must have all been like as children down here."

"We were boys who'd lost our parents. Angry, rebellious, sad. But this place did us good. Gave us something to focus on and taught us how to work well with others."

"But did anyone show you love?"

My question seemed to bemuse him, and he glanced toward Clay, who looked away.

"We had each other," he said eventually. "We were a family of sorts. We looked out for one another."

I figured that was something, at least.

Chapter Fourteen

I wanted to see more of the training rooms, to see what the other facilities were like, and how many boys were living down here, but my aunt wasn't giving off good vibes, and I didn't want to give her any more reasons to be angry with either me or the guys.

"Hey," I said, trying to change the topic. "Can we go and see Lorcan? I'm worried about him."

It was true. After seeing Alex help him into the elevator, he'd been playing on my mind. I thought he was putting a brave face on just how bad he'd really been feeling, and I hoped Alex had been able to help him.

Kingsley nodded. "Sure. The medical bay is on the other side of this floor."

"Yeah," Clay said. "I wanna see how he's doing, too."

My aunt wrapped her arms around her narrow frame. "I'm tired, Darcy. I think I'll leave you to it and go lie down for a while."

I chewed my lower lip, frowning at her in concern. "Are you sure?"

"The bell will go for dinner soon," Kingsley said, his expression matching mine. "You don't want something to eat before you sleep?"

I agreed with him. "You've barely eaten all day."

She waved a hand in the air between us. "I'm fine. Stop fussing and let me get some rest."

I hesitated, unsure what to do. But then I reasoned with myself that she'd been having sleepless nights due to my disappearance, and we'd asked her to walk a fair distance today as well, plus all the traveling. It shouldn't be surprising that she'd be worn out.

"Okay, sure," I relented. I didn't want to admit it, but a part of me was relieved that she was going to lie down. I felt more at ease with the guys without her watching over my shoulder. I knew she was judging every interaction we had with each other, and while I didn't blame her, it was making me, and probably them, too, awkward.

"Well, you know where the dining room is if you hear the bell and decide you've changed your mind," Kingsley said. "Just come on up, and you'll be more than welcome."

She nodded, but didn't meet his eye.

Together, we went back to the elevator, though we remained outside, while my aunt stepped in.

"Are you sure you don't want me to come with you?" I asked anxiously.

"Don't be ridiculous, Darcy. I'm more than capable of finding my way back to the room I've been allocated. Go and see your friend."

I gave her a tight smile. "Okay. As long as you're sure."

She reached out and hit the button for the next floor up, where the bedrooms were located. "Of course, I'm sure."

My insides squeezed with guilt. This was easier for me because I had the guys, but she must feel like she didn't even really have me. The metal doors slid shut, hiding her from view, and then the elevator started to move up, leaving me alone with Clay and Kingsley.

"C'mon, sugar," Clay said, hooking his arm around my waist and yanking me to his side. "Just give her a little space and time, and she'll soon warm up."

"You clearly don't know my aunt."

Kingsley jerked his head in the opposite direction. "Let's go and see how Lorcan's doing."

I was glad to have the distraction.

We walked the length of the corridor until the doors gave way to a glass-walled room at the end. The space was divided into several more rooms beyond, and it was in one of these we found Lorcan. A pole stood beside the bed he was lying on, a bag of clear fluids, which was now almost empty, leading down to a drip threaded into a vein on the back of Lorcan's hand. His eyes were closed, his chest bare. A sheet was pulled up halfway and tucked in just above his navel, and I found myself picking out the individual images of his tattoos—a raven, an eye, some script in what looked like Latin—enjoying being able to look while he didn't know. Like Isaac, I felt Lorcan held himself back from me in a way the other three guys didn't, even though we had shared that kiss. They were more open, emotionally, and I wondered what had happened to Lorcan to make him the way he was. Was he wary of all women, or only me?

Alex walked in, a stethoscope draped around his neck. He wore a white coat over his shirt, and looked every part the young, handsome doctor. My heart fluttered a little, and I had to glance away.

"How's he doing?" Kingsley asked Alex, keeping his voice down so as not to disturb Lorcan.

Alex nodded. "Better. The rest is doing him good, and I've had him on some fluids and IV antibiotics, which will get working right away."

I hated to see Lorcan like this, especially as I felt partway responsible for what he was going through. I wished I could do something to help, but Alex had everything under control.

Lorcan's eyes flickered open and came to land on me. He gave a smile at seeing me at his bedside.

"Hey," I said gently. "How are you feeling?"

He winced and shifted, trying to sit up, but I put my hand on his bare chest. "Don't move. Just rest."

"Yes, she's right," Alex said.

Lorcan frowned. "I'm okay. Alex is being dramatic."

I glanced over at Alex, who rolled his eyes at Lorcan. "The infection hit you fast," Alex said. "But the antibiotics will work quickly as well."

"That's good." I didn't like to think of any of them out of action.

Alex touched me on the elbow and jerked his chin to indicate him wanting to speak with me. I took a couple of steps from Lorcan's bedside, and Alex used his body to shield our conversation from the others.

"Hey, Darc. I wanted to say I'm sorry if I upset you back at the truck stop. I shouldn't have been digging into your business."

I shook my head and glanced away, embarrassed at my over-reaction. "No, it's fine. I just didn't like the thought of you and Clay talking about me in the car."

Alex stared at me, his blue eyes wide. "We didn't. I mean, not like that."

I knew exactly what he meant by 'not like that.' He was talking about the thing I'd been paranoid of—what Clay had thought of me in bed. Alex hurried on, as though the conversation embarrassed him as well. "I mean, I saw you guys this morning, and obviously I was there when Isaac ..." Again, he didn't need to clarify. "So, I just figured it might be something you'd given some thought to, and obviously with our current situation, it's not as though you can visit your regular doctor ..."

I held up a hand to stop him. "It's fine, Alex, though thank you. I know you're just looking out for me."

"In that case, please take this as me looking out for you." He reached into his pocket and pulled something out, though kept the item hidden in his palm. He slipped his hand into mine and released what he was holding. I glanced down to find a folded strip of condoms nestled in my palm.

"Alex!" My cheeks burned.

"Do whatever you want with them—throw them away, if that's what you want—I just wanted to make sure you're taken care of, you know? That you have the choice to be protected, if need be."

I wondered if he was thinking about using the protection with me. Maybe it had crossed his mind, but if that was the only reason he was giving them to me, he wouldn't have bothered. He could have just produced them if, or when, the moment arrived.

I stuffed the foil packets into the back pocket of my jeans. "Thanks, Alex," I mumbled, hoping none of the other guys had witnessed our little transaction.

He seemed happy with that. "Welcome."

There was so much potentially about to happen, I struggled to think more than a couple of hours into the future, never mind something like birth control. But he was being practical and responsible, and that was a good thing.

The shrill ring of a bell sounding from circular speakers in the ceiling interrupted our conversation. I was glad for the distraction.

From Lorcan's bedside, Clay clapped his hands. "Meal time!"

"You guys go." Lorcan waved us away. "Someone will bring me food down."

I felt bad leaving him. "Are you sure?"

"Yeah. You guys woke me, anyway, and I'm more tired than hungry."

My stomach gurgled, acid bubbling. It had been a long time since the breakfast sandwich, and I wasn't a fan of these inconsistent meals. I was normally someone who was already planning what was for lunch as I was eating breakfast.

Still, guilt swamped me as I put my hand on Lorcan's good shoulder and leaned in to kiss his cheek. His skin felt smooth and warm against my palm, and I resisted the urge to lay my head on his chest and hold him awhile. It felt like we were abandoning him. Things never felt right unless the six of us were together. "Get some rest, okay? We'll be back soon."

Alex pointed to a handset beside the bed. "Hit the buzzer if you need anything, and we'll be right down."

Lorcan gave a half smile, but it didn't reach his hazel eyes. He did look tired, and my heart contracted with worry for him. "No worries. Go. Eat."

We all turned and filed out of the medical bay, leaving Lorcan to rest. I wondered how the talks had been going between Isaac and Devlin. Had they decided what would happen next? I knew we couldn't just hide down here. We still needed to find Hollan. We still needed to find the memory stick.

I piled into the elevator with Alex, Kingsley, and Clay pressed in on each side. Kingsley hit the button, and we rose back up to Middle 1, the floor which consisted of the living area.

As we walked into the massive dining room, people were already seated around the numerous round dining tables. The air was filled with the hum of conversation and the clink of cutlery striking plates. I suddenly felt hugely conspicuous, and found myself stepping in behind Kingsley's bulky form, as though to hide from everyone. I wasn't a shy person, but being the only female around made me self-conscious. I spotted a couple of other adults—some of whom I'd watched taking classes with the boys—but most of the inhabitants were below the age of eighteen.

I didn't see Isaac or Devlin anywhere. They must still be busy.

Alex nudged my side and pointed over to a table which was only partially occupied by some of the boys. A buffet of food had been laid out along one wall of the dining room, so we helped ourselves to plate-fuls of macaroni and cheese and a tomato salad, then took our seats at the table with the boys. My mouth watered. The food appeared to be home cooked, and, other than the curry Clay had made, there had been a distinct lack of home cooked meals in my life lately. I wondered how they got their food down here. Did one person go out and do a massive shop somewhere—not that I thought there would be anywhere nearby—or were they growing fresh fruit and vegetables somewhere?

I forked a mouthful of soft pasta smothered in creamy, cheesy sauce into my mouth and chewed, savoring every bite. The tomatoes were ripe and sweet, with torn basil flaked on top to bring out the flavor. It was a simple meal, but delicious, and my thoughts went to both Aunt Sarah and Lorcan missing out.

I swallowed then leaned into Alex eating beside me. "Will someone take a plate down to Lorcan?"

"Yes, of course. He won't go hungry."

"What about my aunt? Should I put something aside ...?" I felt awkward asking. She'd not shown them any gratitude for their hospitality, but I couldn't see her going hungry.

"Of course. I'll make sure we put her a plate to one side so she can reheat it later if she wants."

I smiled gratefully. "Thanks, Alex."

I got the feeling of eyes on me, the heat of a gaze hitting my skin, and looked up. I was drawing attention from the boys as they all sat with their meals. They ranged in age from about seven to seventeen. Some of them looked down at their plates, blushing furiously, while others stared at me openly.

"This must be how Wendy felt when she went to Neverland," I said to Alex from the side of my mouth.

He caught me in his blue gaze. "Yes, but *we* all grow up."

That was true. The boys who'd brought me here were most definitely men.

"You don't get many women or girls down here?"

Alex shook his head. "No, not at all. You're an unusual sight."

I looked around the room at the numerous males. Other than my aunt, I was the only female. "Why are they all boys?" I asked Alex. "Do they not think girls are capable?"

Alex gave a small laugh that contained no humor. "Honestly, it's because the boys were the ones left on the shelves."

I frowned. "What are you talking about?"

"The girls are always adopted, and they're never going to stop a child from going to a loving home if he or she had one. The sad fact of the matter is that a boy is half as likely to be adopted as a girl, and that chance gets even worse as the boy gets older."

My emotions were torn. Should I be feeling sorry for these kids, that they were taken away from the one chance of having a normal family, or should I be looking at these boys as the lucky ones? This might not be a traditional home, but I'd seen how the guys all looked out for one another. Sure, they fought and annoyed one another at times, just like any siblings, but they had each other's backs. And not only that, they were given a profession. Wasn't that better than them growing up in foster care homes and potentially ending up on the streets, with no future ahead of them?

I looked back to the boys. They all appeared happy and healthy. If I asked them directly where they would rather be, would they say here? Or was that because they didn't know any better? If they'd been left in the foster home for just that little longer, would the right family have come along?

Chapter Fifteen

We finished eating, and the boys walked around, picking up empty plates from the tables and stacking them to be washed. The scene reminded me of being back in the house, when we'd finished the curry, and Lorcan had collected the dishes. Had that been his job here, as well? I pictured a ten-year-old Lorcan, sullenly collecting dirty plates, his dark hair falling over his eyes.

Someone walked into the room, commanding attention. Everyone looked, and I followed their gazes, as people tended to do when everyone was looking at one thing, to see Isaac standing in the doorway. He caught the eye of Alex, Clay, and Kingsley beside me, then jerked his chin to tell them they were wanted.

The guys rose from the table, and I hesitated, unsure of what to do. "You, too, Darcy," Isaac called over to me. "This concerns all of us."

My stomach churned, the cheesy pasta suddenly sickly and too filling. I wished I hadn't eaten so much. This would be about our next move, and while I'd enjoyed this small moment of respite, getting to see where the guys had grown up, and learning a bit more about what had shaped them into the men they were, I knew we had a job to do. My fury and hatred at Hollan and what he'd done hadn't abated in the slightest. I still wanted to see him dead, and I wanted him to look in my eyes and see it was the daughter of the man he'd murdered who caused his demise.

My legs felt weak, but I pushed myself to standing, my palms flat on the table to steady myself. I followed Alex, Kingsley and Clay out of the room. The younger boys were watching the older men with fascination, as though seeing their futures walk by. I caught one of the boy's gazes—a red-haired, eleven-year-old, with freckles across the bridge of his nose—and threw him a smile. The boy returned the smile, though a blush made his freckles stand out even more against his pale skin.

Again, I couldn't help thinking about the way these kids lived their lives. Were they allowed outside? Did they get to go to the nearest town and shop or go to the movies? I had so many questions I stored away to ask the guys about later.

We waited at the elevator. The doors slid open again, and we stepped inside and rode the car up. My pulse thrummed, causing my heart to race, and my breath was shallow in my lungs. What would Devlin have to say about what we'd do next, and would I get any input in it?

Devlin was waiting for us as the elevator opened again, depositing us at the upper floor. The men who'd been working on the computers earlier were no longer here, giving us privacy. The screens on the walls continued to show various images, though now the screen that showed where we'd entered only had a dirt ground, felled trees, and rusted equipment on it.

Even though I had the others by my side, Devlin's attention went straight to me, and he smiled, the lines beside his eyes crinkling. He made Isaac look small, and younger than he was. I didn't think there were many people who could make Isaac appear inferior, but this guy managed it.

"Hello, Darcy," he said, flashing me a smile of straight, white teeth. "Thanks for joining us."

I glanced around at the others. Why did I suddenly feel as though this meeting was more about me than anything else? "That's okay. I figured whatever was being said would include me as well."

He nodded. "Yes, you're right. You're very much involved in everything that has happened. Isaac told me you've given us the code to the memory stick, and you should know how grateful we are."

Flutters of unease danced through me. When I'd given Isaac the code, I'd believed I was giving it to the five of them. I hadn't considered someone else being brought into the equation, and a deep sense of regret filled me. I'd told myself the code was my only bargaining tool this whole time, and yet I'd let it go. Had I given it up too soon?

The smile he delivered didn't meet his eyes, and I knew bad news was coming.

"Isaac and I have discussed what's going to happen next, and we've decided it will be safer if you and your aunt remain here, with us."

My jaw dropped, and I shook my head. "Not happening."

"Isaac warned me that you might not be happy about it."

My eyebrows lifted. "Not happy is an understatement. This is the exact reason I didn't want to give over the code in the first place, because I knew I'd end up being sidelined. Just because I'm female doesn't make me incompetent. My dad taught me how to handle a gun, and there are things I can do that you won't have even considered."

I almost told them about my synesthesia, but kept my mouth shut for the moment. I didn't know if I'd be able to use it to my advantage, but I wanted to make sure I played that card at the right time. I was already regretting giving too much too soon, and I wasn't going to make the same mistake twice.

"This isn't a prison, Darcy." Devlin took a couple of paces, his hands behind his back. "We can't stop you from leaving, but just in the same way you want your aunt to stay safe, we want the same thing for you, too."

"That's different. This involves me. My father gave *me* that code, not one of you, and Hollan is the one responsible for killing him." My lips tightened. "I want in on this. I want to find out what's on that memory stick, and I want to see Hollan pay for what he did."

Devlin's jaw went rigid, the square jut suddenly becoming unattractive. "What's on the memory stick has nothing to do with you."

I flashed him a look. "So, you know?"

"Of course, I do. Do you think we'd go to this much effort if we didn't?"

I folded my arms across my chest. "Tell me. Then I might be a little more cooperative."

His cobalt blue eyes narrowed. "You mean you'd stay here, let us deal with things, without giving us any trouble?"

I didn't want to say yes or no. "I'll think about it."

He came to a halt in front of me and folded his arms, mimicking my stance. The muscles of his biceps strained against his shirt. "Sorry, that's not good enough."

I looked back, toward the others, trying to catch one of their eyes and have them plead my case. But none of them looked toward me, each of them finding something more interesting to do—Clay studying the nails of his right hand, Alex scuffing something on the floor with his foot, Kingsley looking behind him. Their lack of support caused pain to ball in my chest. Them not speaking up for me felt like a betrayal, and though I knew Devlin was their boss—and perhaps had been even more to them, a father figure of sorts—it hurt that they weren't standing up to him on my behalf. Didn't they want me around? Were they happy to leave me here and go off and do their own thing?

My aunt's words niggled at me. Had I been too quick to trust?

Emotions threatened to cloud my thinking. They could force me to stay here, if they wanted. They'd done it before, so what was to stop them trying again? At least, while they were still willing to talk, I could get some information from them. The idea of all the guys leaving to deal with Hollan, to put themselves in dangerous situations, while I remained useless here, threatened to fill my eyes with frustrated, angry tears, but I bit the inside of my lip to hold the tears back. This was a male environment, and crying wouldn't help my cause. I wanted them to take me seriously, not pity me.

I turned my attention on Isaac, tried to plead my case with my eyes alone, but he pressed his lips together and shook his head so slightly, I had to wonder if I'd imagined it. I knew what the look said—he wasn't going to take my side either. They all wanted me to stay. I experienced a sudden pang of longing for Lorcan. Would he have taken my side? He was the least conforming of the group, though I doubted things would be different if he were here.

If they didn't want me, I wasn't going to force myself on them.

I swallowed down my anger and pride. "Okay. I'll stay, if you tell me what's on the memory stick my father died trying to protect."

Devlin raised his eyebrows at Isaac, and Isaac nodded his agreement. It occurred to me the men could easily feed me a lie, and I'd be none the wiser.

"Locations," Hollan said. "A series of coordinates, to be exact."

My eyes narrowed. "Coordinates for what?"

"Places like this. Training centers. Bases. All across America. To keep them protected, we don't even know where they are. We work as individual units against corruption."

"You're spies," I interrupted.

He nodded slowly. "In a way, yes, but necessary spies."

"And you don't know where other places like this are?"

"No one does, and that's how it should stay. It's the only way to keep us safe. If one place is infiltrated or corrupted, then we know all the others will remain unharmed."

My brain whirred as I thought hard, trying to put all the pieces of information together and make sure I had it straight in my head. If I was giving up my chance to kill Hollan myself, I was sure as hell going to make sure the information I got in return was worth it. "But the details are on the memory stick?"

"Yes, but they're only supposed to be accessed in case of emergency. Your father understood how important it was not to have that information fall into the wrong hands, and so he took the memory stick from Hollan's possession and put the code on it, the same one he gave you."

My shoulders lifted in a slight shrug. "If no one should know that information, why did you even need the code? Why not just find and destroy the memory stick?"

"Because even though we don't want it falling into the wrong hands, if something happened that affected us all, then we'd issue a code red and the locations would be revealed. Someone would need to coordinate our teams."

My eyebrows lifted. "That someone being you?"

He nodded. "At this point in time, yes. That information has been missing for years now. For all we know, bases like this one might have already been inactivated, or infiltrated and destroyed. Before you gave the interview to that reporter, we believed the information was lost forever, and it didn't matter that Hollan had the memory stick because he'd never be able to access what was on it, and if he even tried, he'd wipe out the contents. But now we know we can access it, and the time has come to make sure it's back in the right hands."

My mind processed everything he'd said. "But surely you'd have someone who coordinated these various groups, so multiple teams don't show up to deal with one situation?"

His lips pressed together, his nostrils flaring. He dipped his head in a slow nod. "We did, before the memory stick was taken. The stick was only ever supposed to be backup, you see. But the man who coordinated us all was killed at the same time as it was stolen, so, other than the memory stick, that information died with him."

I could understand why Devlin and the others would want to know the locations of the other bases, but why would it interest Hollan? "And what does a man like Hollan want with that information?"

Devlin rubbed his fingers across his lips. "Let's just say that us watching over the shoulders of men in power isn't what men in power want."

I frowned. "You're saying they'd want to know the locations of these places to stop you?"

"That's exactly what I'm saying."

"But how?"

Isaac stepped forward, joining the conversation. I had noticed how quiet they'd all been while Devlin had been trying to explain. "You've already seen how Hollan works, Darcy. He killed your father. He sent a team of armed men into the house after us, shooting before asking questions."

The penny dropped. "You're saying he'd find you all and kill you?"

Isaac nodded. "Exactly."

My eyes widened. I imagined how it would be if armed men descended on this place. With it being buried in the ground, there were no secret ways out—at least not that I was aware of. People would fight back, or perhaps they'd run and hide, but this was their home, and they wouldn't be expecting it. It would be nothing short of a massacre. "But ... but ..." I stumbled over my words, my brain trying to process the sheer horror of what might happen. "There are children here."

Kingsley's hand touched my lower back, and I glanced up into his concerned face. "We know that, Darcy. Why do you think this is so important to us?"

I glanced around at the faces of the others. Clay, Alex, and Isaac wore identical expressions to Kingsley, and it dawned on me just how important it was that Hollan never got access to the memory stick.

"People in power don't want us to exist, love," Isaac said. "Before now, we weren't much more than a rumor, a ghost story, something politicians could rib each other about, but with that stick, there is proof. They can track us down and put a stop to us."

"But surely there are people Hollan works with who would stop him from doing that? They can't be all bad!" I thought of my father, and how he had died to prevent this exact thing from happening. He'd tried to get the memory stick out of Hollan's hands, and he'd known how important it was for Devlin and Isaac to have the information, or otherwise he would have just destroyed it instead of placing the code on it."

"We don't even exist," Kingsley said, "not really. The boys being trained have been taken out of the system. You think anyone is going to notice or raise a red flag because we go missing? No one is going to know."

I shook my head in horrified disbelief. "So Hollan would just come in and kill you all?"

Isaac nodded. "Kill those who won't be any use to them, take those who they think will have information."

"But the children ..." I thought of the shy boys at dinner, how they'd blushed at the sight of a woman and stared down at the table. I thought of how Clay, Kingsley, Alex, and the others would have been as boys, and the idea of men being sent in to have them killed filled me with fury. "This is obscene. Surely it wouldn't happen. Someone would put a stop to it!"

"Who would put a stop to it, Darcy?" Devlin asked, his voice gentler than it had been. "We're the people who would normally put a stop to that kind of thing, but if we're the ones being targeted, it would be a whole different thing. We'd be fighting for our lives."

The horror of it swept over me. Military men swarming places like the one we were in now, shooting children as they ran, putting an end to this small task force. What would the military be told? Not that the children were being raised to put an end to corruption, but quite the opposite. The men charged with the job to wipe them out would most likely be told they were dealing with terrorist units, though I couldn't see how they would justify the killing of children. But wars were happening every day, and thousands of children were killed then. Nothing stopped the atrocities.

I clamped my hand to my mouth. "Jesus Christ."

Hollan had to be stopped, and we had to get our hands on that stick. The magnitude of the issue suddenly expanded in my mind, and

I understood the gravity of it. I didn't know what I'd been expecting to be on the memory stick—maybe the names of some important people, or even the location of money, or weapons, but I hadn't been expecting this.

"I want to help." I stared at Devlin earnestly. "I know I can. Put me to work, make use of me. Don't leave me wandering around here with nothing to do."

His full lips twisted, and he shook his head. "No, sorry. I have my team, and they've worked together for most of their lives. You just ... complicate things."

"Lorcan is hurt," I said, feeling guilty for using his injury, especially as it had been sustained because I'd been stupid enough to call Aunt Sarah from the house phone. I wouldn't be dumb enough to make a mistake like that again. "I can take his spot."

Devlin turned to Alex. "How is he looking?"

"Better already." Alex shot me an apologetic half-smile. "The antibiotics are doing their job. I'm hoping he's stronger by morning."

Devlin looked back to me, shaking his head. "Sorry."

I gestured into the air. "So, you'd rather let an injured man go than me? Why? Because I'm a woman?"

Devlin's expression grew darker. "No, because he's had training."

That training didn't stop him from getting shot, I almost said, but managed to clamp my lips shut. I knew I was speaking out of anger, and saying things without thinking them through wasn't going to get me anywhere.

"You think Lorcan will be well enough to leave tomorrow?" Kingsley directed his question toward Alex.

Alex nodded. "He won't be perfect, but he'll be better."

"Great," I muttered, scuffing my foot against the floor.

"And do we have an idea where Hollan is?" Clay asked.

Devlin nodded. "Yes. He must have gotten some info about you leaving the city from the west, so he's been spotted in that direction.

We have eyes on him. What we really need is one of these on him, however." He turned to go to a desk with a computer on it and picked up a small box, which looked as though it would contain a ring or other piece of jewelry.

I frowned at it, but Isaac nodded. "A tracker."

Devlin opened the box and picked out what appeared to be a flesh colored circle, mere millimeters in diameter. He dropped the tracker into his palm then held it out for us to see. "The best available. It presses against the skin and embeds itself, like a tick, but without the blood. It's almost unnoticeable to the wearer—especially if you get it into a fold of skin, like under the arm, or in the hairline. Unlike normal trackers which might go in a phone, or on a car, something that can be dumped by the person you're trying to track, this will be on the person at all times."

Isaac inspected it, frowning. "And you think Hollan will lead us to where he's keeping the memory stick?"

Devlin nodded. "That's the plan."

"We'd need to get close to him," Clay said.

Devlin closed his palm around the tracker and dropped it back into the small box it came in. "I'm aware of that."

Clay pushed his hand through his hair and straightened. "That's going to be dangerous."

"Is that a problem?" Devlin said, setting the box back down on the desk.

Clay scowled. "No, sir."

I hated standing there, feeling useless. I was still hurt from the guys not standing up for me, and now I had to listen to the danger they were going to put themselves in. What if something happened to them when I wasn't there? What if they left, and one or more of them got killed, and it was the last time I ever saw them?

"We leave in the morning?" Isaac asked.

"That's right." Devlin turned away, as though the conversation was already over.

"I should go, too," I blurted, not giving up just yet.

He faced me, his blue eyes cold. "We made our agreement. I told you what you wanted, now it's your turn to behave yourself."

He turned away again, not giving me the courtesy of even looking at me while I had the chance to reply. None of the others told him not to talk to me like that—not that I was expecting them to. I felt like I'd been dismissed like a child, and shame flooded over me. I didn't want to be there, with the guys all knowing they were leaving in the morning on their mission and with me deemed as not being good enough. It was humiliating, and I hated it, and I only wanted to go and hide.

I spun away, pushing past them.

"Hey, sugar," Clay called, but I didn't even raise my head to look at him. Tears threatened, and I didn't want any of them to see, but especially not Devlin and Isaac. They were as bad as each other.

Ignoring everyone, I rushed to the elevator and slammed my hand against the button that would take me down to the floor where the bedroom I had been told I could stay in was located. The elevator felt as though it took forever to arrive, each second that passed only causing my mortification to deepen. What I really wanted was for the guys to tell Devlin they weren't going anywhere without me, but their silence had gone on too long, and however much I wished it would happen, it was only a fantasy. The doors finally opened, and I jumped inside, not even turning back around to face the front of the elevator. I couldn't stand to see any of their faces as the doors slid shut and I gave into the burgeoning storm of tears. Blindly, I stabbed my finger at the keypad, hitting the button for the floor which housed all the bedrooms.

An overwhelmingly childlike desire to be home swept over me. I longed to be able to cry in my own bed, to bury my face in my own pillow, and inhale the comforting scent of home. But I knew that was never going to happen, so instead my thoughts went to my aunt, still sleeping, I assumed.

A part of me wanted to go and cry on Aunt Sarah's shoulder, but I knew she'd tell me she'd been right all along.

Chapter Sixteen

I found the room I'd been allocated and burst into it, throwing the door shut behind me with a bang. The space was cold and impersonal, and again I longed for my own bedroom at home. I wished there was something more I could have done or said to make them see me as more than just some girl. At least when I'd had the code, I'd been something special. Now I was a no one.

You should have told them about your synesthesia, a little voice whispered in my head. *Then they'd have taken you seriously.*

Would they, though? What use was it, really, other than making me good at remembering numbers and dates?

A gentle knock came at the door, and it opened before I had the chance to say to either come in or go away. I didn't know how I felt at that moment—filled with impotent rage, knowing I wanted to do something, but finding the wall I came up against to be steep and impenetrable.

Kingsley's face appeared through the crack then he stepped fully into the room. "Hey," he said, his brows pulled down in concern.

Using my sleeve, I wiped at my face. "Hey."

I hated that I'd been crying, though the tears had been from frustration and anger more than anything else.

He gestured to the bed. "Mind if I sit down a minute?"

I didn't want to be pleased that he'd come down to see if I was okay, but I was. I wanted to still be mad at him and tell him to go away, but these were crazy times, and deep down I was happy to see him.

I shrugged. "Why the hell not? It's not as though this is even my bed." I lifted my hands. "None of this is mine, or under any of my control. You can do whatever you like." I dropped my hands in helplessness.

His weight depressed the mattress as Kingsley sat beside me. He reached out and took my hand between his two, far larger ones, pressing my fingers between the warmth of his palms. "You know we never meant for you to feel that way."

I lifted my eyebrows, but I didn't pull my hand away. I wouldn't say it out loud, but having him here did make me feel better. "No? You guys kidnapped me and locked me in a cellar for three days. It feels like everything that's been done has been to take away my control."

"This will all be over just as soon as we get our hands on that memory stick and use your code."

"And what happens to Hollan?"

"Don't worry about him. He'll be taken care of." The tone of his deep voice suggested he wouldn't be taken care of in a good way.

"And I'm just supposed to hang out here like a good little girl and wait for it all to be done for me?" I wanted to bite down on my bitterness, but it oozed from every word like resin.

He twisted on the bed to fully face me. "Shouldn't that be a good thing? Aren't you sick of running and fighting?"

I shook my head. "Are you?"

"This is all I know. I was raised for this."

I caught his deep brown gaze, staring into his eyes to try to get across how earnest I was. "In a way, so was I. My father knew who I was, every detail about me." I was thinking about my synesthesia and how he'd chosen me to tell about the code. "He trusted me. Leaving it to others makes me feel as though I've failed him."

A hint of a sad smile tugged at his full lips. "No, Darcy. You could never have failed him. You're smart, and brave, and ridiculously beautiful. You remembered the code, despite everything. You could never have failed him."

As Kingsley spoke, he moved closer, the inches between us on the bed vanishing. The atmosphere between us changed, and my breath stuttered in my chest. I sniffed, feeling as though I was looking far from my best, but the action only caused Kingsley's dark eyes to soften.

He lifted his hand, releasing mine, and placed his fingers to my cheek. "I meant it when I said you're crazy beautiful, Darcy. I know this isn't a perfect situation, but you have to know that I, or any of the guys, would be crushed if anything were to happen to you. It's only been a week, but you've gotten under our skin. All of us. I see how the others look at you, too. You don't need to be a shrink to see they care."

I gave a small laugh and pressed my cheek deeper into the warm cup of his palm. "Even Isaac?"

"Yeah, even Isaac. I know he's not the easiest of people to get on with, but he means well."

I lifted my hand to cover the back of his. "And what about you, Kingsley? Do you care, too?"

"You know I do. I don't need to say it. You can see it in the way I look at you."

He was right. The depths of his eyes held something deeper, and my heart fluttered in my chest. Kingsley was big and intimidating, at first glance, but I thought perhaps he was the softest of all the guys. He was the first to have shown me any kindness back in the cellar, and with the thought came the memory of how his hands had felt massaging my back, and my nipples tightened in response. I'd masturbated after that massage, imagining how it would feel to be with someone as huge as Kingsley, and right now, from the way he was looking at me so intently, I thought he was wondering how it would be for us, too.

I inched closer, my lips parting, and I pulled his hand away from my face and kissed his fingertips instead.

"Darcy ..." His voice was hoarse.

"It's okay," I encouraged.

And it was. It felt right. Kingsley had looked into my mind, he'd protected me when I'd needed it, had healed me with his touch. Now I wanted more, and so did he.

He pulled his hand from my grip, and his mouth replaced his fingertips, his full lips warm and firm against mine. My hand snaked around the back of his head, my fingers digging into his tight, coarse curls. Our lips parted, tongues sneaking out to touch. The moment they did, the kiss grew deeper, and excitement pulsed through me. His tongue pushed more fully into my mouth, flicking across my teeth, and I kissed back with equal force.

My breathing came faster, and I pushed forward, all but crawling into his lap. He grabbed the backs of my thighs and pulled me onto him, so my legs looped around his hips and I found myself straddling him. His hands dug into my hair as our kiss deepened further, his tongue pushing into my mouth, and mine finding his. His hips lifted, and I ground down, feeling the length of his cock press against my pussy, the material of our clothing keeping us separate. I felt his frustration at us still being clothed, but I didn't think it would stay that way for long. His biceps closed me in, bunched muscle containing huge strength. He could probably crush me in those arms, but he was the gentlest of them all, his touch seeking my acceptance at every level.

My hands slipped down his neck and across the muscles of his back. I didn't want his shirt in the way, and when I reached the bottom, I shoved my hands under, eager to make contact with his skin. Despite the hardness of him, his skin was impossibly soft, contrasting against the hardness of muscle beneath. Like a blind man, I traced every inch of the skin of his back, but I wanted to see more of him. I pulled away a fraction, creating space between us, and my fingers fumbled to the buttons of his shirt, trying to unfasten them with a haste that made me clumsy.

I finally managed to unhook each button from its hole, and I pushed the material from his broad shoulders, allowing it to fall onto the bed behind us.

He was built like something I'd only ever seen on television in some kind of superhero movie. How was it possible for him to have a body like this, and not spend every second in the gym? Sure, I'd noticed he'd needed more food than the others, but the man was like a work of art. His chest was smooth and free from hair, his skin glued to the squared blocks of his abs. His navel dipped down, and a line of tight black curls led beneath the waistband of his pants.

Kingsley wasn't interested in my admiration of his body. He was far too busy peeling off my t-shirt, dipping his mouth to the hollow of my collarbone and tracing it with his tongue.

"God, Darcy," he murmured. "You're so damned beautiful."

"So are you," I said truthfully.

His hands went to my back to flick open my bra. The underwear loosened around my shoulders, and he peeled it away, freeing my breasts. He looked down at me, his dark eyes hungry with desire. He ducked down, leaning me back, supporting my weight with his strength. His mouth closed around one nipple and he pulled it into his mouth, rolling the tightened bud with his tongue. The action drove me crazy, and I moaned, shoving my hips against him, seeking more.

He held me easily at my back with one hand, while his other hand reached to my pants. Deft fingers popped the button, and he slid his big hand down the front of my jeans and into my panties. The space was tight, but he managed to angle his hand so it cupped my pussy beautifully. He'd already watched Isaac do this to me. I guessed he figured now was his turn.

His fingers slid me open while his mouth continued to work on one nipple before moving onto the other, his teeth teasing me into two hardened peaks. My breathing came fast, and he moved his finger in a 'come-hither' gesture, pushing inside me.

"Oh, God," I gasped, pulling back up toward him to decrease the space between my breasts and his chest, "that feels so good."

He lifted his face from my breast and we kissed again, a flurry of hungry mouths. I ground down on his hand while I was still seated in his lap. Then I reached for him, feeling the hard ridge down the front of his pants. I wasn't as coordinated as he was, and yanked at his belt then fumbled with the button until he used his other hand—the one that wasn't inside my pants—to undo himself.

I caught his cock in my hand the moment he came free. He was so big, my fingers not even meeting around his girth. "Holy shit."

I pumped his length a couple of times, both marveling at his size and trying not to be a little intimidated by it. My strokes along his erection caused a groan to issue from between his lips, and I loved hearing him make that sound.

"It's okay." His breath was hot against my ear. "I can make it easier for you."

He slipped his hand from my panties and flipped me onto my back on the bed. Then he grabbed the ankles of my jeans, yanking them from my hips, together with my underwear, and throwing them to the floor.

I half sat up, propping myself on my elbow. "Wait," I said. "Check the back pocket of my jeans. There's something I think we're going to need."

Kingsley gave me a curious glance, and then reached back down to the floor and hooked my jeans up. He checked the pockets and found the condoms Alex had given me earlier. He held them up like a prize then dropped the jeans back to the floor.

I was naked in front of Kingsley. Utterly naked. He placed the condoms down on the night stand then stood at the edge of the bed and shucked his pants from his hips, and undid the rest of his shirt, leaving him as naked as I was.

Fucking hell. He was magnificent. The chocolate brown of his skin shone with sweat, highlighting his muscles. His body was relatively free from hair, except for that small buzz down to the thatch around his cock. The bed dipped as he climbed onto it. His big body eclipsed me, and he lifted my feet and wrapped them around the back of his head. Then he dropped down, his face between my thighs, and his mouth met with my hidden folds. He licked me from the base right to the top, and I gasped as his tongue curled around my clit, before dipping back down again. I arched against him, a moan crawling from my throat. God, that felt incredible.

He made me soaking wet, from my own arousal and his saliva. His hot tongue met with my clit, sending instant sparks through me, and my back lifted from the bed. He brought me so close to the edge, licking me with a tongue that was surely as big as the rest of him, until I was a writhing, squirming bundle of nerves.

Kingsley sat up, leaving me gasping. He leaned back on his heels, and his hand went around his dick. He stroked it from top to base a couple of times, my eyes glued to the motion, then reached for the packet of condoms Alex had given me. He tore one off and opened it with his teeth. He removed the condom and slowly rolled it down his thick length.

My eyes widened at the sight of him, and either he was good at picking up on my reaction, or he'd had this experience with a lot of women. That slight twinge of fear in my eyes that he just might not fit.

"Just relax, Darcy. Breathe and this will feel so good, I promise."

I was soaking wet from when he'd gone down on me, and I did trust him that he wouldn't hurt me.

I nodded, and reached for him. "Yes, I want you." The corner of his full lips pulled in a smile that told me he knew I wasn't about to say no.

This wasn't just physical. I felt we had a mental bond as well, from all the times he'd hypnotized me and guided my mind with his words. He'd led me on a journey, with only his voice to direct me, and I'd trusted him to do that. I'd felt bonded with him then, and us being together now only felt like the physical progression of what we'd been through.

He supported his body over mine, and I hooked my feet around his hips, urging him toward me. His cock pushed at my entrance, and I tensed momentarily, but then felt myself open around him. Kingsley nudged with his hips, pushing inside me, inch by inch, stretching me. His body felt amazing, and I clung to his shoulders, his skin soft in contrast to how hard he felt.

He inched in until he was buried, balls deep, inside me. We stilled liked that for a moment, and he kissed me again, slow and intense, while my body grew used to him. Stretched, and full, and perfect.

Kingsley began to move inside me, his hips meeting mine until we reached a slow but deliberate momentum. Each stroke set every nerve ending alight, and I forgot everything else, only how it felt to be with this incredible man. My body focused on climbing, building toward the climax I knew was coming. I'd already been so close when he'd had his mouth on me, and it wouldn't take much more to bring me back to that precipice.

His breathing became primal groans, and he fucked me faster, his hips pistoning against mine. I squeezed my eyes shut as the heat in my pussy spread upward, the muscles of my belly tightening in anticipation. My toes curled, and everything exploded around me. Kingsley drove into me a couple more times before holding himself deep, his face buried in my hair and the side of my face.

The rigidness of his body went loose, and he dropped down gently and rolled to his side, careful not to crush me.

His fingers knotted in the ends of my hair, and he stared down into my face with an almost stunned bewilderment at what had just happened. "Fucking hell, Darcy. That was amazing."

My heart began to slow, and I smiled. "Yeah, it was."

We curled in together, him pulling me so my back pressed against his chest, and his arms wrapped around me. I felt safe here, cocooned within his embrace, and as I felt sleep trying to claim me, I tried not to think about how I'd feel in the morning when they all left.

Without me.

Chapter Seventeen

Confusion and anxiety filled my dreams. Numbers danced in front of my face, and I knew I was supposed to have remembered which order they needed to go in, that it had been crucially important, but none of them would stay still. They darted around like lightning bugs, and the positions certain numbers always took in my surrounding space were all wrong. Instead of number one being the closest, it was number nine, and normally I saw eight behind one, but now it was four. Seven should be right in the center of my vision, but that had been replaced by five. It was all wrong, and, to make matters worse, none of them would stay in the same place.

"I trusted you, Darcy," my father's voice said, and I looked up to find him standing in front of me. Behind him were the patio doors he'd been shot through, and I frowned at them in confusion. Hadn't he been shot already? How did I know the number if he wasn't already dead?

But I didn't know the code, did I? I'd gotten it wrong, and that was why I couldn't get the numbers to stay in one place.

"We trusted you, too," said Alex from behind my back, and I turned to find all five men standing behind me. They each wore identical expressions of disappointment.

Kingsley pressed his full lips together and shook his head. "Now you've forgotten it, haven't you? If you'd just told us right away, we wouldn't be in this position."

My mind blurred. "But I've already told you what the code is. You already know!"

He shook his head. "No, you didn't. You've been keeping secrets from us, and now you've forgotten the code, and it's lost forever."

I didn't understand what was happening. I'd told them, hadn't I? Unless that part had been a dream and the code was still locked inside my head. But the trouble was that the numbers weren't inside my head. They never had been. They were dancing around me, and they wouldn't stay still.

I blurted it out to Kingsley.

Isaac stepped in. "What are you talking about, Darcy? Is this something else you haven't told us?"

My dad joined in, and I cowered away, feeling ganged up on. "What happened to you, Darcy? You used to be such a good girl, and now it's all lies, lies, lies."

"No, that's not true." I shook my head, frantic.

"You've let me down. You're such a disappointment to me, and to your Aunt Sarah, too. It's a good thing I'm dead, because otherwise I don't think I'd have been able to live with you in my life."

A spot of blood suddenly appeared on his chest and started to grow. But he didn't react to it, just stood there, shaking his head at me as the red spread, taking over his entire chest.

And behind me, the guys echoed his words ...

Such a disappointment.

I WOKE GASPING AND coated in a sheen of sweat. The sheets clung to my body, and my heart thumped. It took me a moment to piece together the events of the last few days and realize it had only been a dream. It had been horrible, but my first fear was that I'd forgotten the code again. I was still able to see the numbers, wasn't I? I visualized the code my father had given me and exhaled a sigh of relief when the numbers popped up in my vision, as clear as they had been when I'd gone to sleep.

Despite having already told Isaac and the others what the code was, I refused to allow myself to forget it again. Not that I wanted to consider the possibility, but if something happened to them, I'd be the only other person who knew it, though I assumed Isaac had given it to Devlin. But perhaps he hadn't. Maybe Isaac was keeping it back, too, making sure they were kept on this assignment. It had been my only piece of leverage, and now it was theirs.

I realized something else. Kingsley was no longer with me.

What time was it? Had he left to get ready for the day? Or had he sneaked out not long after I'd fallen asleep, seeking the solitude of his own bed? The thought of him leaving weighed heavy on my heart for some reason. I'd have preferred it if he'd stayed with me. Between my legs felt slippery from where we'd had sex, and I had that low pleasurable ache from being fucked good and hard.

I pressed my fingers to my lips, holding back my smile. Even if Kingsley had left, that didn't change what we'd done together. Being with him had been something I definitely wanted a repeat performance of. I wondered if he'd tell the others. Would he and Clay compare notes? Would they all discuss how it felt to have their fingers inside me? Poor Lorcan would most likely still be in the sick bay, and I wasn't sure how close Alex and I had gotten. We'd spent the night in bed together, but I still wasn't completely sure what had happened, if anything. It might have all just been my imagination, dreaming as vividly as I did. Did my vivid dreams, which I'd had since I'd been a child, have something to do with how suggestible I was when I was under hypnosis? Were all those things perhaps linked to my synesthesia—my mind working in a different way than others?

Guilt filled me, but it wasn't to do with not having told them about my synesthesia yet. No, I'd just remembered I'd given no thought to my poor aunt next door. I hoped she hadn't heard Kingsley and me last night. She already suspected there was something going on between me and the guys, and I didn't know how she'd feel if she knew I wasn't exactly being selective about any one of them. It felt right to me, and I got the impression they felt the same way, but I didn't know how someone on the outside would view things. Aunt Sarah could be a little judgmental at the best of times, and, with everything else going on, she was bound to not approve.

Still, I felt bad that I'd abandoned her in her room, even though she'd said she wanted to be alone. I should have told her that I'd had food put to one side for her. I'd meant to, but then I'd gotten caught up in Devlin and Isaac's plans to shut me out, then Kingsley had come to see me and I'd forgotten everything else.

Getting up, I used the adjoining small bathroom, then pulled my clothes back on—they still lay on the floor where Kingsley had thrown them. I opened the bedroom door and poked my head out into the corridor beyond. Seeing no sign of life, I slipped out and went to the room next door where my aunt had taken herself to rest. I knocked lightly with the backs of my fingers. "Aunt Sarah? It's Darcy."

I paused, listening for movement beyond. Surely she wouldn't still be sleeping? A buzz of worry zinged through me. I hoped she was okay.

I knocked harder this time. "Aunt Sarah?"

Again, I got no reply, so I reached down and tried the handle. It turned smoothly, and the door swung open to reveal an empty room beyond. She'd remade the bed. I frowned. Was she in the bathroom?

Stepping more fully into the room, I crossed the floor to the adjoining door of the bathroom. Again, I knocked, but got no response, so I turned the handle and pushed the door open to reveal a tiny bathroom identical to the one I'd just left. But there was no sign of Sarah.

I glanced back at the bed. I'd assumed the bed had been remade, but maybe she'd never slept in it?

Worry escalated inside me. Yes, she may have gone up to try to find some breakfast, but I doubted she'd have done so without me. Maybe she'd heard Kingsley with me last night, and had thought it best not to disturb me, not wanting to embarrass any of us.

With concern pushing at my back, I left the room and hurried to the elevator—not quite at a run, but certainly a fast trot. There didn't appear to be anyone around, and I found the solitude unnerving. Where was everyone? Had something happened while I'd been sleeping, and no one thought to wake me?

I punched the button on the elevator to take me to the living quarters. My anxiety bubbled like acid in the back of my throat. I didn't know what I imagined, but I didn't like it. I hopped from one foot to the other, willing the tin box I was stuck inside to hurry up.

Though only seconds had passed, it felt like forever. Finally, the doors slid open, and I rushed out, pushing through them before they'd even opened fully. A blast of voices and activity hit me, the smell of bacon and coffee lingering in the air, combined with something acrid and sharper—burned toast.

I spotted Kingsley's broad shoulders, standing talking to someone. He must have sensed me approaching, and glanced back over his shoulder. His lips tweaked in a small smile, but I didn't return it.

"You're awake," he said. "You were sound asleep when I left, and I didn't want to disturb you."

I didn't care about that any more. "Where's Aunt Sarah?" I scanned the people sitting at various tables, or lining up to help themselves to the breakfast buffet. I spotted a couple of the guys—Lorcan was out of the medical bay and was sitting with Clay. They both saw me, and Clay lifted his hand in a wave, Lorcan nodding. I returned a tight smile, and I saw the expression on Clay's face change when he realized something wasn't right. I couldn't let myself be distracted by the guys, however, and I continued to search the small crowd. Aunt Sarah wasn't among any of the people here.

Kingsley dipped his head to bring himself to my level. "What are you talking about?"

I bit my lower lip, my teeth tugging at a piece of dried skin. "She's not in her room. I went to check on her, and she wasn't there. She's not here, either, and I'm not even sure if her bed was slept in."

"I'm sure she's around here someplace." But a frown marked his brow, and he cast glances off to either side as though expecting her to materialize. He looked back to me and placed his hand on my shoulder, to either steady or reassure me. "Wait here."

"No way. I'm coming with you."

I was sick of everyone telling me I needed to wait behind, so I followed Kingsley over to where Clay and Lorcan were sitting.

Kingsley stopped beside their table. "Hey, have you seen Darcy's aunt? She's not been seen since before dinner yesterday."

I should have asked Lorcan how he was feeling, but my mind was caught up in a whirlwind of possibilities. They didn't know how she'd been thinking. In their minds, she was on our side, but I knew differently. She hadn't really trusted Isaac and the others, and thought I might be making a mistake.

Clay shook his head. "Nah, sorry, man. Not seen her since she went to lie down yesterday."

"Where are Isaac and Devlin?" I asked. "They might know."

Clay lifted his stormy gray eyes to the ceiling. "On the top level, making preparations for us to leave today to go after Hollan."

I frowned. "And Alex?"

Lorcan spoke up. "One of the younger boys had dislocated a finger as I was leaving. He stayed down in the sick bay dealing with the kid."

Could my aunt have gone there? Had she gotten ill in the night and gone to find help? Why hadn't she come to me first—had it been because I'd had Kingsley in the room with me?

I looked to Lorcan. "Did you just come from there? Did you see my aunt?"

He shook his head. "Sorry, princess. No sign of her."

I forced myself to ask after him, not wanting them to think I was caught up in my own little Darcy bubble, where I was incapable of considering someone else. "You're feeling better, though?"

Lorcan gave me a rare smile, and my heart melted a little for him. It was good to see the tense, pain-filled expression he'd sported all the previous day had vanished. "Yeah, much. I can help you look."

"Only if it's not going to make you worse."

He shrugged, then winced as the movement obviously caused him pain. "Devlin is already planning on sending me back out on the job today. I'll be fine."

Kingsley straightened. "I suggest we go and speak to Isaac and Devlin. Find out if they know where your aunt has gone."

Clay and Lorcan rose from the table, leaving their breakfasts half eaten. In an unspoken agreement, we all headed toward the elevator. As we stepped inside, and Clay hit the button for the upper level, I had the horrible thought that Devlin and Isaac might have picked up Sarah's reluctance to be here and done something about it. Would they hurt a woman if they thought she was a threat to them? It seemed crazy, but then this whole thing was crazy. They'd gone as far as kidnapping me, hadn't they?

The doors slid shut, encasing us inside the metal box.

Could they have done something to Aunt Sarah?

Chapter Eighteen

The elevator doors slid open to reveal Devlin, Isaac, and several other men who worked the computers and surveillance equipment. They all appeared busy, mostly focused on computer screens, while one was on the phone. They had the air of important men doing important things. I didn't give a shit about any of that, though. I only wanted to find out one thing.

I marched straight up to Devlin, and he looked to me in surprise. "My aunt is missing. I'm not sure she slept in her bed. You know anything about that?"

"Your aunt?" He shook his head. He did appear genuinely confused, but he might have been a good liar. "No, I haven't seen her since you first arrived."

"You sure about that?" I challenged.

His blue eyes narrowed a fraction, causing fine lines to span out in crow's feet from the corners. "Of course I'm sure. Why would I lie?"

"Because you did something to her."

His eyebrows lifted, looking at me as though I might have a screw lose. "And why would I do anything to your aunt?"

"I'm not sure, but I'm trying to figure out a reasonable explanation why I can't find her anywhere, and it's not as though she has anywhere she can actually go."

Devlin's lips twisted and he glanced over at the men who were working on the surveillance equipment. "Hey, Sinclair, you were on watch last night, weren't you?"

A tall, slender man with red hair, who I guessed to be in his thirties, straightened from the screen he'd been watching. "Yeah, boss. I'm due to finish my shift any minute now."

"You know anything about Darcy's aunt missing?"

He shook his head. "Nope, sorry."

"But you were watching the screens all night?"

He nodded, but then frowned, his teeth digging into his lower lip.

"What is it?" Devlin demanded, taking a couple of steps toward the other man. He'd obviously sensed something wasn't quite right.

Sinclair hesitated, as though he wasn't sure if he should say something. I stepped forward as well, joining Devlin and decreasing the distance between myself and the other man. "Please," I begged, "if you know anything, tell me. She might be in danger."

Or be a danger to us, I thought, but didn't say.

Sinclair spoke. "One of the younger boys, William, came up here last night."

"He did?" Devlin snapped. "Why? The boys know they're not allowed on this level."

"He wanted help with a project he was working on down in the science lab—an electrical circuit they were supposed to have produced by the next day—but he was struggling with it. It was late and he said he couldn't sleep because it was worrying him so much. He begged me to go down and help him, just for five minutes, so I did."

Devlin seemed to grow bigger in his anger, his back straightening, his shoulders becoming broader. "You left your post?"

"Only for five minutes—ten, tops."

Devlin shook his head then ran a hand through his hair. "Go and get William. Let's see what he has to say for himself. I'm not aware of the boys having any projects like that going on right now, and he certainly shouldn't have been disturbing you when he should have been sleeping."

Sinclair bobbed his head in a nod, and hurried to catch the elevator down to where the boys were probably still eating breakfast.

While we were waiting, Devlin headed to the security screens. He brought up the screen which showed the outside area, and began to scroll back through the time. The night vision was black and white, and a little grainy. Devlin kept scrolling, going back in time to the previous evening. As he did so, my synesthesia caused a timeline to flash up in front of my eyes, scrolling to the left in time with Devlin.

Most of the screen showed nothing more than the external, rusted machinery, and some fallen logs, but then movement flashed across it.

"There!" I stabbed my finger at the screen. "Go back."

Devlin did as I asked, and slowed down the footage.

The person crossing the screen wore a hoodie pulled up over their head, hiding their face. From their height and shape, and just the way the person moved, I knew it was my aunt. "That's her."

"Dammit. What time was that?" Isaac asked.

Devlin frowned and leaned in to check out the small clock on screen. "A little before eleven."

My heart sank. That had been hours ago. She could be miles away by now.

The elevator opened behind us, and I twisted to see Sinclair emerge holding a boy—William, I assumed—lightly by the shoulders, more to steer him than force him forward.

The boy's head was down and tears streamed down his face. He was one of the younger boys—around eight-years-old. My heart tightened at the sight of him, hating that he was in distress, but we needed to know what had happened.

Sinclair nudged William on the shoulder. "Tell them what you just told me."

William wiped the back of his hand across his nose, leaving a pale, silvery trail across his skin. "The lady, Sarah, asked me to help her. She said she needed to make sure her family was safe, and this was the only way she'd be able to leave."

Had she meant me when she'd said she needed to make sure her family was safe? Did Aunt Sarah think by leaving and getting 'help' from Hollan, that it would be helping me?

Devlin asked the next question. "You helped her by distracting Sinclair?"

The boy's voice broke in a sob. "My mom's name was Sarah, too. The lady made me think of her, and I couldn't tell her no."

"Hey, it's okay," I said, trying to offer the boy some comfort, even though my stomach twisted at the idea of my aunt using a small boy in this way "There's no harm done, is there, Devlin?" I glared at the older man, trying to tell him to let the kid off with no more than a warning. This hadn't been his fault. Kids did what adults told them to—especially these kids. He wasn't to know she shouldn't be trusted, and the idea that my aunt had reminded him of his mother made my heart break.

"We'll talk about this later, William," Devlin said. "Class will be ready to start soon."

The boy sniffed, and nodded, but seemed relieved to be able to run back to the elevator and sink back down into the bowls of the earth, away from all the angry adults.

I rounded on Devlin. "So my aunt was just allowed to walk out of here? All it took was distracting one of your security team?"

Devlin's lips pinched. "This isn't a prison, Darcy. You're all free to come and go as you please. We keep an eye on the boys, of course, but we don't make people stay here who don't want to."

"You have codes on the outside door and cameras everywhere!"

"The code on the hatch is to keep people out, not keep people in, and the cameras are for outside, too. This place is a home as much as anything else, and we're not in the business of making the people who live here feel like they're being spied on."

I could barely believe what I was hearing, especially after I'd been kept captive myself for a number of days. It wasn't as though they were averse to doing that if necessary. Something inside me tripped uneasily. Was I advocating holding my aunt here against her will? Wasn't that doing to her exactly what they had done to me? But it was to keep her safe, I told myself. Trouble was, that was exactly what the guys had used to justify the way they'd taken me and held me captive.

I'd simply assumed we wouldn't be allowed to leave here of our own free will, but maybe Aunt Sarah had never made that assumption.

"Shit!" I thought for a moment. "Could we try to use the computers to try and spot her now?" Isaac had used satellite imagery to watch over my house before we'd gone there to get Aunt Sarah. I knew they had the technology.

He shook his head. "There's too much tree coverage around here. It works well for the cities, but assuming she's left the clearing, we won't be able to see if she's walking down the side of the road. The canopy overhanging the road is too dense. And we definitely wouldn't be able to tell if she's managed to get a ride from someone. She could be in any kind of vehicle."

We were in the middle of nowhere. Would she have tried to walk to somewhere she felt safe? Would she have tried to take one of the vans we'd passed parked nearby when we first arrived? A crazy thought—Aunt Sarah stealing a vehicle. I would never have previously thought her capable of such a thing, but now I wondered.

A second thought occurred to me. Had she brought her cell phone here? She'd managed to keep hold of her bag even when we'd had to change cars in the tunnel, even when I'd forgotten mine. Was there a reason she'd clung to it so tightly?

"Oh, shit." My stomach contracted with anxiety.

Isaac must have seen the expression on my face, as his own complexion paled. "What is it?"

"I'm worried she might have used her phone to contact Hollan."

Isaac's head darted back in surprise. "Why would she do that?"

"You have to think from her point of view for a moment. She's known Hollan for years. She trusted him."

"You're her niece," he pointed out. "She was supposed to trust you, too."

His words made my eyes fill with tears, and I blinked them away. "I think she still sees me as that crazy, irresponsible teenager she had to take care of. She doesn't realize I grew up. She was fed Hollan's side of the story first, and I guess he painted me as being spontaneous and reckless, maybe choosing to leave with you guys instead of being taken. And then she picked up on the connection between us all ..."

I didn't want to say any more than that. Devlin was in the room, and what happened between me and the guys was none of his business.

But Devlin had been listening to every word, and he stepped in, his face rigid with anger. "God damn it. You were brought here because your connection to your father meant you weren't considered to be a security risk, and now you're saying your aunt was on Hollan's side all along, and possibly has just walked out of here with a cell phone, ready to contact him and give him our exact location?"

My eyes filled with tears. I should have told them what Sarah had been thinking, but I'd wanted her to be on our side so badly, I'd kidded myself that she was coming around to our way of thinking. After everything I'd told her, I'd never considered that she would take Hollan's side. Did she really think Kingsley had put the memory into my head of me seeing Hollan on the night of my father's murder? She must, if she didn't believe me at all.

Isaac stepped to my side, his presence supporting. "We have to try to find her." He looked to me. "If she has her cell phone, can't you call it?"

My teeth caught my lower lip and my cheeks flushed with heat. "Yes, of course. Dammit." I didn't know why I hadn't thought of that already. I clearly wasn't thinking straight. The digits of her cell phone flashed up in front of my face in spatial sequence. Calling her now might be too late, however.

"She might have contacted Hollan already," I said.

Devlin's head twisted in my direction. "You think she'd give up the location of this place?"

My blood ran cold. I wanted to convince myself she wouldn't do that. She'd seen there were children here, hadn't she?

Isaac's lips thinned, his nostrils flaring. "She's your aunt, Darcy. You vouched for her. You made it sound as though we could trust her."

My eyes welled with angry, frustrated tears. How many more mistakes was I going to make? How many more times would I get everyone in trouble?

Devlin jerked his head. "Get on the phone," he told me.

Feeling sick, I hurried over and picked up the handset. I punched in the numbers as they appeared in front of me, then pressed the phone to my ear. *Please pick up,* I prayed, but it didn't even ring and instead went straight to her voicemail.

"It's me, Aunt Sarah." I caught the guys watching, and shook my head to indicate I was talking into a machine rather than a person. "I'm sorry you felt you had to leave without speaking to me, but please, please don't go to Hollan. If you love me at all, you have to trust me on this. It's literally a matter of life and death. I love you."

I didn't want to tell her we were coming to find her. I thought that if she'd reached Hollan, it would only give them time to prepare to face us.

I put the phone down to find multiple gazes locked on me.

Gesturing out either side, helplessly, I said, "I can't do any more from here."

Isaac nodded his agreement. "We're going to have to go after her."

"We don't go out without being prepared," Devlin commanded. "You take everything we'd already set up for today."

I straightened, putting my shoulders back and lifting my chin. "I'm going, too."

Devlin put his hands on his hips. "No, you're not. This is about our security now as much as protecting your aunt. We need to bring her back in."

I held out both hands. "I get it, I do, but this will all go down a lot smoother if I'm there, too."

Kingsley stepped in beside me, and I glanced up at him, grateful to have his solid presence. The back of his hand brushed my fingers, and I resisted the urge to grab hold of his hand and hang on tight. "She's right," he said. "Darcy and her aunt are close. I'd rather we're able to have a conversation and persuade her to come back than having to use physical force right away."

I hated to think of my poor aunt being manhandled into the back of a truck.

Devlin shot me a look. "They couldn't have been that close."

His words were like a knife in my side. I knew what he was saying—that if we'd been close, she would have believed me instead of taking off. And I knew the reason his words hurt so badly was because they were the truth. I couldn't blame her, though. I'd been the one who'd spoken to the reporter in the first place. I probably couldn't be trusted.

Behind us, the elevator doors slid open, causing us all to spin around. Stupidly, I hoped it might be my aunt, but instead Alex's form was revealed, and he stepped out into the room.

"Hey," he said, glancing around at our anxious faces. "What have I missed?"

Isaac filled him in. "Darcy's aunt vanished during the night. We think she might have had a cell phone with her, and that she's contacted Hollan and left. Apparently, she didn't believe what Darcy told her about Hollan being the one responsible for killing her father."

Alex winced and looked to me. "Shit, sorry, Darc."

I shook my head, brushing off his sympathies, though I did appreciate them.

"This is my fault." I resisted adding 'again,' knowing they'd kept the story of the last time I'd messed up—when I'd called my aunt from the house—from their boss to protect me.

I had one final card to play, and I figured now was the right time. I turned to Devlin, fixing my gaze on his to show I wouldn't be intimidated. "Let's consider something for a moment. If my aunt is going to meet Hollan, and we're able to find my aunt, then chances are we'll find Hollan as well. Correct?"

He nodded. "Yes, that's more than possible."

I continued. "And where we find Hollan, we also stand a good chance of finding the memory stick. You said the memory stick contains lists of coordinates, right?" Devlin's eyes narrowed at me, probably wondering where I was heading with this, but he nodded. "What would happen if either he or one of us got access to the stick, but it was destroyed before anyone had a chance to make a note of the coordinates?"

"Well, they'd be lost forever." From his tone, I could tell he was still unsure.

"Exactly. But what if someone had managed to see them before that happened?"

"They'd need to have a photographic memory to be able to remember them all perfectly."

"Or a mind that was able to visualize numbers."

He shook his head, unsure. "What does that mean?"

I tried again. "It means I'd be able to remember those coordinates, if it came down to it."

"What makes you think that?" he said, frowning. "I heard Kingsley had to work with you several times to get the code for the memory stick."

I lifted a hand. "First of all, that was completely different. I was fourteen years old and my father was dying. Secondly, I'm good with dates and numbers. I would be able to remember those coordinates if I saw them."

His eyebrows lifted. "Good, as in you did well in school?"

"Don't patronize me, Devlin. I mean good, as in I have a special affinity for them."

His nostrils flared. "Special affinity?"

Seeing that tiptoeing around the subject wasn't getting me anywhere, I jumped in with both feet. "Have you ever heard of synesthesia?"

My change of topic had thrown him. "Synesthesia?" He was parroting everything back at me. His fingers touched his lips as he thought. "Yeah, I've heard of it. It's when people see certain months as colors?"

I nodded. "Right. But that's only a part of it. There are certain types of synesthesia which people hear of more regularly—the popular kinds—and those include the example you just said, but there are others. It's automatic and involuntary. The brain picks up on something and flips it into something else. Some people might see certain letters or numbers as set colors, like the number two might always be pink for them, or the letter S is always red. My brain works in a similar way, but for me I *see* numbers around me, in my personal space." I waved my hand around my head to demonstrate what I meant. "The numbers one to ten are always in the same place for me."

I felt the other guys staring at me, their questions so far unasked, but mentally pressing at me through the space between us. There was a reason I never talked about my synesthesia, and that was mainly because it was so damned hard to get people to comprehend it.

Devlin frowned, and I could tell he was trying to understand, even though I knew it must sound crazy to him. "Like in order." He pointed to imaginary numbers in front of him and ticked them off with a jerk of his finger, one by one. "One, two, three, four ..."

But I shook my head. "No, they're not in order. The number one is closest to me, but that's where it ends. Eight is behind the number one, and then it's three. Seven is right in front of my eyes, but further away, and nine is beside that. Zero is the furthest away and to my right." I pointed in the direction of zero to demonstrate, though I knew he wouldn't be able to see anything.

I was aware of time passing, and that every minute was another minute Aunt Sarah may have gotten farther from us and closer to Hollan, but it felt vital that they understood. It was a final, weak grasp at trying to get the men to see I was more than a weak woman they needed to protect, and instead someone with skills and strengths of her own.

Isaac joined the conversation, and sounded as confused as Devlin. "But if you need to think of lots of numbers, and they all need to go in an order, like a phone number, how do you know which order they go in if they're always in the same place?"

"They light up, growing brighter and more defined, as though they're saying 'look at me.'"

Lorcan stared, one eyebrow pulling down quizzically. "You know this sounds nuts, right?"

I shrugged. "I can't help it. It's just the way I am."

"And so when you remembered the code your father gave you," Kingsley said, "you saw the numbers in front of you, all lighting up in the order they needed to be?"

I smiled, pleased that at least Kingsley sounded as though he was starting to get it. "I can see them now, if I want. All I have to do is think about it."

"But hang on a minute." Isaac lifted a hand. "If it came down to it, we'd need to remember coordinates, not single digits."

I nodded. "I can do that. My synesthesia comes in other ways as well. For example, I see dates as well, both my past and my future. They're like a slide running across my vision. My present is directly in front of me, and my past heads left and, where I can no longer remember, vanishes behind me on my left," I gestured in that direction to demonstrate. "The future goes the other way and where I can no longer see any upcoming dates or events, vanishes behind me to my right."

It all made perfect sense to me, but I looked around at all the guys' faces to see that it wasn't quite so clear to them. I'd stopped telling people about the way I saw things partly because of the expressions on the guys' faces now.

I gave a sigh. "You've got internet access. Google it."

Alex lifted both hands. "No, no need for that. We believe you. I've heard of synesthesia before, and I'm sure Kingsley has, too." He looked toward the bigger man.

Kingsley nodded seriously, his eyes never leaving my face. "Of course, I have. It's more common than we think, but people just don't talk about it. They either don't realize other people don't see the world that way, or they've already had reactions from people thinking they're crazy, so they've stopped talking about it."

I nodded, knowing exactly what he meant. Despite knowing my aunt was missing and there was a good chance she was headed to Hollan, my heart somehow felt lighter now I'd told them. It wasn't as though my synesthesia was a secret or anything, but I wanted to share everything with these men, and being a synesthiate was a big part of who I was.

Kingsley looked to me with fresh curiosity. "Could your father do what you can do?"

I shook my head. "No, it didn't come from him."

"So, your mother, then?" he questioned. "Synesthesia is normally inherited from the mother or father."

I shrugged. "Yeah, maybe. I don't really know. She didn't stick around long enough after I was born to let me find out."

His face pinched. "Shit, Darcy. I'm sorry."

I let my shoulders lift to try to show them how unbothered I was. "Doesn't matter." The smile I plastered to my face didn't reflect how I truly felt inside. "Can't miss what you never had, right?"

I suddenly realized who I was talking to. Each one of them had been made orphans as children, and here I was bitching about my wayward mother, when I'd at least had my dad to raise me until I was fourteen, and then my aunt after that. They'd all grown up, first in a foster care home, and then in some kind of training institute that I didn't yet fully understand. They'd had no one, when I'd at least had my aunt to take care of me. I'd still grown up in our family home. I hadn't been raised by strangers.

"Shit, sorry." I lowered my face to my palm, hiding my eyes. "I can't believe I just said that. I'm sure you all missed your parents like crazy."

"Hey, it's okay, Darc," Alex said. "We all experienced loss. It all sucked. There's no need to worry about thinking if any one loss was worse than another."

I gave him a thankful smile. "Anyway, what I'm trying to say is that if you need someone to remember those coordinates, I'm the girl for the job."

Devlin had been watching our conversation without interruption.

He leaned back against his desk, his palms on the surface, and exhaled a sigh through his nose. "I'm not going to pretend this doesn't all interest me, but we're supposed to be going to get your aunt, Darcy. We don't know that we'll even come across Hollan or the memory stick."

"But if you do, you're going to want to have me around."

"Only if you get hold of the memory stick and have to access it for some reason."

"Like if the memory stick is going to be destroyed and you need someone to remember the coordinates. Isn't it best to have a backup?"

"We could download them onto a computer or take a photograph with a cell phone," he pointed out.

I shook my head. "Not if there isn't time, or we're in a situation where there is no cell phone or computer."

"If there's no computer, you won't be able to access the memory stick in the first place."

I took a breath, trying to compose myself, gritting my teeth. Why the hell wouldn't he just give in to this? "Okay, well, what if it's Hollan's computer we're using, and there's no other way to transfer the data?"

The men exchanged glances.

Kingsley lifted his eyebrows at Devlin. "She's got you there."

"All I'm trying to say is that I have abilities that will be put to better use out there than hiding in here, and that's before we even get started on the fact that it's my aunt we're going after, and that she's far more likely to come back if I can talk to her sensibly rather than a group of men aiming guns at her head."

"I think she'll come back if we're all aiming guns at her head," Clay pointed out, and I shot him a glare.

Devlin sighed again. "Okay, you can join the men." He jabbed his index finger in my direction. "Don't make me regret it."

I shook my head, trying to hold back the elation that rose inside me. "I won't." I shouldn't be happy at the idea of having to track down my aunt and possibly face Hollan again, but I was.

I just hoped we'd reach Aunt Sarah before Hollan.

Chapter Nineteen

Isaac took charge, giving everyone instructions. "We need to leave ASAP. We don't know how far she might have gotten, or even if Hollan has picked her up already."

"She might not have contacted Hollan," I said hopefully. "She might have just thought she'd had enough of all this and be heading home." If she hadn't taken one of the vans we'd arrived here in, then she would have walked. She was a physically fit woman, but that would be a hell of a walk.

"If she hasn't, we'll pick her up along the way, and hope no harm has come from this."

I swallowed hard. No harm, meaning the location of this place hadn't been compromised by my aunt. Right now, the remaining Sullivan family wasn't proving to be too hot on security.

Packs containing necessary equipment—new weapons, ammo, cell phones—had been laid out for the men, and they each went to collect them. I watched Isaac swipe up the small tracker Devlin had shown us the previous day and deposit it in his pocket.

"Stay in touch." Devlin placed his hand on Isaac's shoulder. "I want to know as soon as there are any developments."

Isaac nodded, his expression stern. "I will."

We caught the elevator again, all six of us crammed into the small space, squashed shoulder to shoulder. Above us, the hatch lifted automatically, allowing the metal box to rise out of the ground. The doors opened, and we stepped out into the cleared logging area, blinking in the bright light. Insects buzzed around my face, and I batted them away. It always felt so strange to be back in the fresh air and sunshine when I'd spent any time beneath ground—as though the rest of the world had ceased to exist. I took a deep breath of forest air into my lungs and looked around in case there was a chance Sarah had been sitting up here, just out of sight of the cameras, all this time. But she was nowhere to be seen. Instead, the beauty of the forest struck me with an almost visceral emotion. The trees around us were heading into fall leaves, an oil painting of reds, yellows, oranges, and browns. I wanted to run between the tree trunks, lose myself in the innocence of nature, and forget everything that was happening, but I couldn't.

Had she started walking in the dark, or had she waited until first light?

I prayed it was the second option. It would be far easier to catch up if she'd only managed to get a few miles down the road.

We set off at a fast walk, following the cleared track back down the hill and around the corner, toward the gate with the warning sign nailed to it. Isaac led the way, while Clay and Alex flanked me, Lorcan not far behind, and Kingsley bringing up the rear. Everyone moved with purpose, and the men had lost the more relaxed attitude they'd had while we'd been in the base. Now they were on high alert again, their fingers never far from the grips of the guns they'd been supplied with. They were watching out for an ambush, in case this had all been a way of luring us out.

Despite the obvious tension, I felt better now that it was the six of us again. This felt right, the way we were together. Even though my stomach was twisted in knots, having the five of them with me helped to make me believe things would come right again. We'd find Aunt Sarah and get her to believe me, whatever the cost.

I didn't like to think about what we'd do if she refused to take our side. The betrayal of that hurt more than I wanted to give thought to.

We passed through the gate, and the pointless fence that only went on a few feet on either side. All the vehicles, minus the van that had delivered us, were still there. So, my aunt hadn't managed to steal one, though the thought had seemed ludicrous. That could be a good or a bad thing. Either Sarah won't have gotten far, or else she knew someone was coming to give her a ride.

Isaac pulled a set of keys out of his pocket. Devlin must have given the keys to him while we'd been back at base. "We'll drive back in the direction we came from and hope we spot her on the road," he said, heading to the driver's door of a van similar to the one we'd arrived in. Dried mud was splashed up the sides of the bodywork, and it looked every bit a workman's vehicle.

Clay went to the rear of the vehicle. "She might have managed to get a ride with someone passing by."

Isaac shrugged. "Possibly, but you don't get many cars on this road."

"My aunt also isn't in the habit of hitchhiking," I pointed out.

I couldn't picture Sarah walking down the road with her thumb sticking out. I doubted she'd accept a ride from someone who pulled over and offered either. She had a suspicious nature.

With Isaac driving, I rounded the front of the van and climbed into the passenger seat to join him. If anyone was going to talk down my aunt, it would be me. I wanted her to see my face first and see how much worry she'd put me through. The others all piled in the back, and then the doors slammed shut behind them.

Isaac started up the van, and I sat up straight, leaning forward, craning my neck, as though that would make her more visible to me. I longed to spot her sitting on one of the felled tree trunks, a disapproving expression on her face, and her explaining to me how she'd felt claustrophobic and simply had to get out of there. I didn't think that was going to happen, however.

We bumped and jolted over the uneven terrain, until we were back on the road again. Isaac drove slower than normal, aware we might come across Sarah walking down the side of the road. It wasn't as though there were sidewalks all the way out here. The road gave way to forest on either side, a blanket of fallen, brightly colored leaves blurring the edges between nature and manmade.

Clay leaned forward from the seat behind and placed his hand on my shoulder, giving me a squeeze. "We'll find her, sugar. She can't have gone far."

I didn't want to take my eyes off the road for a second, so I covered his hand with mine and squeezed back in return. I sensed the tension radiating off Isaac—nothing new for him—but everyone else had been good about Sarah leaving. None of them had berated me and made me feel it was my fault.

Because we'd made the journey here in the back of the van, and I hadn't been able to get a good look at the road, the route we took now was unfamiliar. We also seemed to have the road to ourselves, and on the rare occasion a vehicle passed us in the opposite direction, I found myself staring into the windows of the passing car, picking out its inhabitants and wondering if I'd see my aunt with them.

The longer we spent in the van, the more miles we put between us and the base. My fears that Hollan had picked her up increased with every mile we covered. I questioned myself the whole time, wishing I'd done things differently. If only I'd paid more attention to her. If only I'd gone to see her after dinner, instead of running to my room and taking comfort in Kingsley's arms instead.

"She couldn't have gotten this far on foot," I said, shooting Isaac a worried look.

"She could if she left last night."

I shook my head. "She'd be exhausted. I don't think she's physically capable of walking this far."

"People can surprise you when they're under pressure."

I didn't reply, but inside I knew he was wrong. I knew my aunt. She might have walked some of it, but if she had her phone on her, she would have called someone to come pick her up, and chances were that person had been Hollan.

The road became narrow and winding, and, to my frustration, Isaac slowed down the car.

We were never going to find her at this rate.

Chapter Twenty

We rounded a curve in the road, and Isaac slammed on the brakes, throwing us all forward. The seat belt jammed across my shoulder and breasts, punching the breath from my lungs, and automatically I put out my hand to save myself from hitting the dashboard. Cries of surprise and a grunt of pain—which I assumed originated from Lorcan—rose from the guys behind me.

Catching my breath, I looked up to see what had made Isaac stop so suddenly. Several vehicles waited in the road— expensive-looking black cars, identical to the ones that had picked me up at my house all those days ago—and in front of the vehicles were a number of people. My heart crawled up my throat, and every muscle in my body tensed.

They'd known we were coming. They were ready for us.

Hollan stood in front of the cars with his arm around my aunt's throat, the muzzle of his gun jammed against her temple. He was a short man, but, despite his height, was powerfully built. Sarah looked terrified—her eyes wide behind glasses that were skewed on her face, her skin pale. Her fingers clutched at Hollan's arm around her neck, but she made no move to try to pull his arm away. The gun was enough of a threat to prevent her from doing so.

I clamped my hand to my mouth. "Oh, God."

My worst fears had come true. Hollan had reached my aunt before we had. How had she been so stupid? She must have called him as soon as she'd left the base. I berated myself as well. I should have done more to make sure she didn't leave. It had just never occurred to me that she would take this route.

I couldn't change the past, but I could make things right again.

Instinctively, I reached for the door handle, but Isaac's fingers wrapped around my upper arm, holding me back.

I yanked back on him. "What are you doing?"

"If you go out there," he said, his voice controlled and level, "they'll take you. The only reason they haven't started shooting already is because they know you're in the van and they can't risk hitting you instead of one of us."

"But I can't just leave her!"

His hand remained tight around my arm, our faces only inches from each other. "She showed her alliances, love. Sometimes you have to know when to let people go."

I shook my head. "No. Sometimes you have to know when not to give up on people."

I leaned in and pressed a kiss to his lips, catching him off guard. I felt his body relax, responding to my kiss, despite the armed men in front of us. It wasn't the type of hungry kiss I'd shared with Clay, or Kingsley, or Lorcan, but instead was soft, gentle, even chaste. With Isaac distracted, I slipped my hand into his jacket pocket and pulled out the box he'd placed in there before leaving.

Our lips parted, and his gaze studied my face, trying to read me, wondering why I'd kissed him. Did he think it was my way of saying goodbye?

I lifted my hand—the one not holding the box I'd stolen from him—and placed it to his cheek, the feel of his stubble rough beneath my fingertips.

"Hollan will take me to the location of the memory stick," I said. "Just take care of my aunt, okay? She didn't understand what she was doing."

Confusion flickered across his handsome face. "What?"

I didn't need to say anything more, knowing he'd soon piece things together. Instead, I turned from him and grabbed the handle of the passenger door and shoved it open.

Isaac reached for me again, but I was ready for him this time. Isaac wasn't the only one to try to stop me leaving, and Clay grappled for me from behind the seat, but I moved too quickly, darting out of reach.

"Darcy, no," Isaac growled at me through the open door. "What are you thinking?"

The voices of the others chased me out as well.

Alex called, "Darcy, wait!"

"Stop!" Kingsley commanded.

"What the hell?" was Lorcan's angry comment.

The sound of them wrung my heart dry. I didn't want to leave them behind. Hell, it was the absolute last thing I wanted, but I couldn't see this situation ending any other way. If I didn't do this, things could go badly wrong. I'd already been responsible for Lorcan getting shot. I wouldn't allow another person to be hurt because of me.

My feet hit the asphalt of the road, though I kept the van door between me and Hollan and his men in front. I was out fully now, crouching beside the vehicle. I felt sick with nerves and my hands trembled, but I had to do this.

Knowing Isaac and the others could see what I was doing, I flipped open the box I'd taken from Isaac. The view of my actions was hidden from Hollan by the open door, but I knew the guys were able to see, and, gently, I plucked the tiny tracker out of the container and dropped it into my palm. I threw the empty box back into the van and quickly pressed the tracker into the skin of my hairline, not far behind my ear. Isaac's eyes widened at me, and then looked down at the empty box. He knew exactly what I'd done, and that had been my intention all along.

"Darcy..." he said.

I shook my head, my eyes wide. "I have to do this. You'll be able to find me again."

Moving slowly, I rose from behind the door. All the moisture had sapped from my mouth, and I rolled my tongue, smacking my lips together to try to swallow. As well as the men and cars in the road, I spotted my aunt's bag, which she'd taken from the house, thrown onto the grassy verge.

There was a cry of alarm as I put myself in full view, though I was unsure if it came from my guys, my aunt, or Hollan's team. The men aimed their weapons right at me, but Hollan put up a hand. "Don't shoot the girl!"

I put up both hands as well. "I'm unarmed, Hollan. Let my aunt go. There's no point in taking both of us!"

Hollan frowned. "What do your friends back there think of you just handing yourself over?"

"They're not happy about it," I called, "but what can they do? This is my decision, and they know you're going to start shooting if I don't, and someone else is most likely going to end up shot. One of them is still suffering from the gunshot wound he sustained the last time we fought."

Hollan's eyes narrowed and he looked suspiciously toward the van containing the five men. He knew they weren't fighting hard enough for me, but I couldn't see any way of changing that. It would only take one shot for everyone to react, and then this place would end up as a bloodbath.

"They'll get me back again," I told him, hoping that speaking plain truth would work on his ego. "And they trust me enough to know it doesn't matter what you do to me, I won't give you the code."

That seemed to make up his mind. He jerked his head toward me, and two of his men lowered their weapons a fraction and started to approach me.

I took a couple of steps back. "Let Sarah go first!"

Hollan scowled, but he released my aunt and shoved her forward.

"No, Darcy!" she cried, reaching for me. "I'm so sorry I didn't believe you."

She clutched at me, just as Hollan's men caught me by my arms. They shoved her away, and there was a moment of grappling—me reaching for her, them pulling me in the opposite direction, while pushing her away. I heard shouts of anger from the guys still in the van, and I prayed they wouldn't try to step in now. They'd ruin everything if one of them started shooting. Tears streamed down Aunt Sarah's face, and the sight of them caused an ache to spread through my chest. It was a rare thing to see my aunt cry. I could probably count the number of times on one hand, and most of those had been after my father—her brother—had died.

"It's okay, Aunt Sarah," I called out to her, trying to reassure her, even though I was the one having to leave with Hollan. "Go to the guys. They'll sort this out."

My heart tore at the thought of being separated from them all. I wished I could have hugged each of them goodbye, imprint the feel of their arms around me one last time, so I could recall their embraces when things got hard. But I told myself this wouldn't be for long. They knew what they were doing, and I had the tracker on me—one Hollan wouldn't find. Hollan would take me to wherever his hideout was, and then he'd get me to break the code on the flash drive.

He wouldn't know Isaac and the others would be right behind us.

Aunt Sarah stumbled in the direction of the van containing the guys, almost losing her balance. Isaac had climbed out of the driver's side, and, cautious of the armed men still pointing their weapons, leaned out and reached toward Sarah. He took her hand and pulled her with him behind the door of the van. I was grateful to him for that small act of kindness, drawing her in, bringing her into their protection, even though she had put us all in jeopardy. The others tugged her into the back with them, and I caught sight of her putting her hands over her face, and Alex rubbing her back. My heart tightened in my chest, and my eyes burned with unshed tears. I wished it was me in her place, but I'd made my choices, and now I had to follow them through.

Find the memory stick.

Kill Hollan.

Those were my plans.

Clay had climbed into the passenger seat which I'd recently vacated, and he stared out at me, our eyes meeting. I would have given anything to be back in that van, to have the guys all around me, but, for the time being, I was on my own. I hoped that simply through eye contact I could tell him I'd be okay, and that, no matter what, I wouldn't give Hollan the code.

Chapter Twenty-one

Hollan's men tightened their hold on me, one on each side, their hands wrapped around my upper arms, their fingers digging into my flesh. I knew there would be bruises there the following day—identical sets of fingerprints.

I could feel the eyes of the others burning into my back, and I prayed they would let me go. Isaac was smart enough to understand my plan, and he'd make sure the others went along with it, however hard it must be for them to watch me being hauled away by Hollan's henchmen.

"Search her, Stewart," Hollan commanded when we reached the cars.

One of the men—Stewart, I assumed, though I didn't know if that was his first or last name—released me momentarily, while the other kept hold of my upper arms. It didn't matter—I wasn't planning on running. I gritted my teeth as Stewart moved to stand behind me.

"Get your hands on your head," he snapped.

The second man who still had hold of me, and whose name I hadn't yet learned, yanked my arms up, and I complied, lacing my fingers on the top of my skull, bringing my elbows out in a V. I was tempted to jab at one of the men with my elbow, venting my hatred toward them, but I knew it would only cause me trouble.

Stewart started at my shoulders, running his hands down one arm, and then the other. The tiny tracker I'd placed in the hairline behind my ear suddenly felt huge, as though it had grown tenfold and was flashing to be noticed. But the man didn't check my hair. He finished checking both my arms, and then shoved his hand into my armpits, before moving to the front of my body. He slid his palms down from my collarbone, reaching my breasts. I clenched my jaw as he ran his hand over my chest, stopping to cup both of my tits, before heading further down. He kicked my feet apart and frisked my legs, running his hands down and back up to brush his palm over the juncture of my thighs, making me tense.

I pictured the expressions of the guys as they watched this happening to me, how furious they would be, and I hoped none of them would let their anger overcome them and do something rash and stupid.

"She's clean," Stewart said, rising back to his feet. He was lucky I hadn't kicked him in the face.

They pushed me toward one of the cars. Two more armed men stepped in to fill the spot the men who now had hold of me had created. They kept their weapons trained on the van containing the guys. They didn't need to, but I wasn't going to tell them that. I needed to be taken for this to work, and the guys weren't going to put up a fight, even though they might want to.

We passed Hollan, and I shot him a glare. "You son of a bitch!"

"You left me with no choice, Darcy. I hope you can see that."

"What about my father? Did he not leave you with any choice either? I know what you did that night. I remember it all now."

"Your father was a fool."

Emotion boiled inside me. "You were supposed to have been his friend!"

"I was his friend. I tried to bring him in on something important, and, instead of running with it, he got all self-righteous on me. If he'd just left things alone, none of this would be happening now."

"You mean if he hadn't tried to protect the people who were trying to keep men like you out of positions of power." I spat the words. It seemed crazy that we were having this conversation now, standing out on the road, surrounded by armed men. Over the past week, I'd played how this conversation was going to go a million times in my head—all the clever, cutting things I would say to him, to make him see what an evil bastard he was, and make him regret everything, right before I put a bullet in his head. Of course, there was no chance of me shooting him in the head right now. Even if I didn't have two of Hollan's men holding my arms, Devlin had never supplied me with a weapon back at the base, and I'd never had the one I'd deposited there when we'd first arrived returned to me.

The men holding me continued to push me toward the back of the car, and Hollan walked alongside us, as though he'd been waiting for this conversation for some time, too, and didn't want to let go of it just yet.

"Ah, so you know all about them now, do you?" he said. "I wondered how much they would have told you. I'm surprised, to be honest, Darcy. They're normally such a secretive group. It must have taken a lot for them to tell you."

I struggled against the men holding me, though I had no intention of breaking free. "They know who they can trust. Unlike you."

He gave a cold laugh. "Don't you mean unlike your father? He was the one who trusted the wrong people."

I shook my head. "No, that's where you're wrong. You were the one who trusted him. You were the one who mistook him for being as corrupt as your sorry ass, and when he didn't go along with your plans, you killed him. But he had the last laugh, didn't he? Six years later, and you still haven't been able to access the memory stick."

We reached the back of the car, but instead of opening the rear door, as I'd thought would happen, I found myself shoved face first against it. My chest slammed against metal, and my arms were yanked behind my back. Hollan took over, the two men stepping back to give him room. I could have fought at that moment, could have tried to run, but there would be no point. Running wouldn't help get the memory stick back from Hollan and into the right hands.

The clink of metal came from behind me, and I stiffened as cold bracelets were placed around my wrists and squeezed together, too tight to be comfortable. The son of a bitch had handcuffed me.

He leaned in and spoke close to my ear from behind. His breath heated my skin, and I caught a whiff of stale coffee. "But all of that changes now, Darcy. You think you won't crack, but we've made grown men break down within hours."

Hours. Would the guys reach me before then? They couldn't follow too close behind, or Hollan would get suspicious. But the idea of being tortured caused ice shards to pierce through my veins. I wasn't a fan of pain. I wasn't the kind of girl who got everything pierced or tattooed and laughed at the idea of it hurting. Fear tasted like a blanket of iron across my tongue. Would the guys take Sarah back to the base, or somewhere else safe, before they came to get me? If so, they'd already be a couple of hours behind. I hoped they were being kind to her, and not making her feel worse than she most likely already did. I was sure Kingsley and Alex would be gentle with her, but Isaac and Clay, and maybe even Lorcan, might not be so forgiving.

I prayed I'd done the right thing by taking this action.

Hollan turned back to shout toward the occupants of the van. "If we catch so much as a glimpse of you anywhere behind us, trying to follow us, I promise you'll start finding pieces of this little lady on the road. Got it?"

I didn't hear any kind of response from the guys, but I was pretty sure Hollan had got his point across. Of course, Hollan didn't know they wouldn't need to keep sight of the cars to be able to follow us.

Yanking me back by my arms, Hollan pulled me away from the car. One of his men opened the rear door, and I found myself being shoved into the vehicle. With no use of my hands, I fell face first onto the seat, my rear in the air. The ungainliness of the position made me feel more vulnerable than ever, and I squirmed to right myself to a seated position.

I'd hoped they'd have left me alone, but to my frustration and anger, Hollan slid onto the seat beside me. He caught me glaring at him, and lifted the corner of his jacket to reveal his handgun in its holster. "I know you're handcuffed, but just in case you get any crazy ideas …"

I scowled at him.

In the front of the car, the two other men climbed in. The man called Stewart was behind the wheel, and he started up the engine. I stared out of the window as the car pulled away, leaving the guys and my aunt behind us. I watched them grow smaller in my vision, until we rounded a corner and they vanished out of sight completely.

I prayed that wouldn't be the last time I'd see them.

Huddled in the back of the car, I was unable to keep the trembling from my body. My extremities felt cold and numb, and I knew my body had rerouted my blood to my vital organs, understanding that in this position of severe stress, the most important thing was to keep my heart and lungs going.

I imagined what would be happening in the van right now. The men would be fighting, for sure. Isaac would be explaining what I'd done, and what my plan was, while Clay would be filled with passionate fury, puffing himself up and gesturing in the direction Hollan had left with me, telling Isaac they needed to go now. Kingsley would be calmer, rationalizing everything, while Lorcan would most likely be joining Clay's anger, but by internalizing it, his jaw rigid and hazel eyes hard. Alex would be taking care of Aunt Sarah, making sure she wasn't physically hurt in any way.

The second car followed us, each vehicle as imposing as the other, as it ate away the miles. I had no idea where we were going, or how long it was going to take to get there, and I swallowed back my tears, blinking hard to keep them at bay.

I missed the guys. It felt like a piece of me was gone.

But they were coming to find me. I knew they were.

I just had to survive until they did.

THE END

LIKED WHAT YOU READ? 'Decoding Darkness' will be out on the 27th of December 2017! Check Amazon for the pre-order which will be up soon!

Acknowledgments

First of all, huge thanks to everyone who has read book one 'Hacking Darkness'. I've been blown away by the success of the book, and it's only encouraged me to write more and work harder to bring you the best possible story I can!

Thanks as always to my long time editor, Lori Whitwam, for making my words shiny, and also not minding when I message her to get me out of a plot hole I'm stuck in! I wouldn't be able to do it without you! Thank you to my proofreaders on this book, Tammy Payne and Karey McComish, for catching those annoying typos!

Many thanks to Daqri from Covers by Combs for creating the fantastic covers for the series. You know I luuuurrrvvvve them!

Finally, thank you to you, the reader, for sticking with me on this journey.

Thanks for reading!

Marissa. XXX

About the Author

Marissa Farrar has always been in love with being in love. But since she's been married for numerous years and has three young daughters, she's conducted her love affairs with multiple gorgeous men of the fictional persuasion.

The author of thirty novels, she has been a full time author for the last six years. She predominantly writes paranormal romance and urban fantasy, but has branched into contemporary fiction as well.

If you want to know more about Marissa, then please visit her website at www.marissa-farrar.blogspot.com. You can also find her at her facebook page, www.facebook.com/marissa.farrar.author or follow her on twitter @marissafarrar.

She loves to hear from readers and can be emailed at marissafarrar@hotmail.co.uk and to stay updated on all her new Reverse Harem books, just sign up to her newsletter! https://landing.mailerlite.com/webforms/landing/e2x3e1

Also by the Author

The Monster Trilogy:
Defaced
Denied
Delivered

The Mercenary Series:
Skewed
Warped
Flawed
Judged

The Spirit Shifters Series:
Autumn's Blood
Saving Autumn
Autumn Rising
Autumn's War
Avenging Autumn
Autumn's End

The Serenity Series:
Alone
Buried

Captured
Dominion
Endless

The Dhampyre Chronicles:
Twisted Dreams
Twisted Magic

The Flux Series
Flux
After Flux

The Blood Courtesans Vampire Romance:
Stolen

Contemporary Fiction Novels
The Second Chances
Dirty Shots
Cut Too Deep
Survivor
The Sound of Crickets

Dark Fantasy/horror novels:
Underlife
The Dark Road

Printed in Great Britain
by Amazon